Sophy

Sophy

Dilys Owen

FREDERICK MULLER LTD

*First published in Great Britain 1974 by
Frederick Muller Limited, London, NW2 6LE*

ISBN 0 584 31115 X

Text set in 11/12 pt. Photon Baskerville, printed by photolithography, and bound in Great Britain at The Pitman Press, Bath

With love to my parents
OLWEN and EDWARD BINNION

Author's note

When I was a child I fell under the spell of an old house, a mansion house that (by the time I knew it) had become a semi-ruin. Hens roosted in the dark corridors; pigs wandered in the muddy morass that had once been a garden and lawn; the orchard, the greenhouse, the kitchen garden had all disappeared, though I have spoken to people who remember them. Now, even the building itself has been demolished, and not a stone of it stands.

This house was called Brymbo Hall. It stood on a high ridge overlooking the distant town of Wrexham in Denbighshire (the "town" in the story). I always wanted to write about it, but no ideas would come, however hard I tried to make it live and fill it with people. I had almost given up hope. And then, one dark January day, I sat down and began the story of Sophy . . .

The diary of Sophy Roy, 1855

PART ONE

January 31st

The wind is quiet today. Instead, there is a cold bitterness over everything. No snow, but a sharp, iron-hard frost. The ground rings like an anvil to the horses' hooves. The sky is nearly touching the top of the poplars along the drive. It is a dull, leaden grey.

I am sitting by the window of the White Room, wrapped up in two shawls and three flannel petticoats. There is no fire here, and my hands are cold and stiff. Only the glass is between me and the frozen garden.

But apart from my frozen fingers, which don't really matter, I am quite warm. I had a sudden fancy to sit here to write. The room is dull, reflecting the grey light from the garden on its white ceiling. It looks very large and very empty. Impossible to believe it could ever have been full of flowers and music, that the door in the hall could be left open onto the terrace. The thought of having the door open makes me shudder, and nothing is so sad as an empty ballroom on a day like today.

But am I sad? I don't believe I am, even though the day is so bleak. I am full of hope, even while I am describing the grimness of my surroundings. If God was angry with me, surely I would never be able to feel like this.

Robert is coming along the drive on the pony. He has been to town for letters. He looks very cold, wrapped up to the ears in his greatcoat and muffler. He is not looking this way, or I would wave. He is huddled over, staring at the ground.

I like to think of the pony as safe in the stable, warm and well-fed, and all the other animals sheltering against the cold. And we are all safe here at home, too. I am warm in my flannel petticoats and shawls, and the baby is warm inside me, we are keeping each other warm. And soon, there will be hot tea and toast by the library fire—for me but not for you, baby.

What does it feel like, I wonder, before one is born?

I hope it might be a girl. I am going to call her Elvira, because that is my favourite name. She can be like my little sister—the one I never had. If it is a boy, I suppose it might look like Charles. I hope not. But I will not call it Charles, anyway, I will call it John, after Father.

Molly is calling me for tea. I must go, or the toast will be cold.

February 1st

Last night it snowed. The lawns and gardens are covered with a thin layer of white, and white light was reflecting into my room when I woke up. This is the first real snowfall of the year.

I went to look out of the White Room windows and saw birds hopping on the wall and the lawn, looking for food. They were very dark against the white snow, and looking so cold. I begged some crumbs and bread from Molly and went to feed them, and then I went to see the pony. She was warm and comfortable in her stall, with heat coming out across the stable door and the smell of hay and horse in the dark corners. There were footsteps criss-crossing in the snow of the yard, where Robert and Molly had been out before me.

After I had seen the pony, I came in and had luncheon, and then I came in here. And that is the sum total of my adventures today. Perhaps keeping a diary was not a very good idea, as there will be few exciting things for me to record. This morning was quite as exciting as any I am likely to experience.

Perhaps I will write a work of fiction along with my day-to-day doings. How daring of me to think of such a thing! I heard

Father talking the other day about a young lady (I think she is quite a lot older than me) who lives in the wilds of Yorkshire, and who has written three or four sensational novels. Her name is Miss Brontë (you pronounce it "Brontay"). Her stories are about mad women and wild, dissolute gentlemen in Yorkshire. I would never be able to write about things like that, of course, but I could write the story of how I was lured away at my coming-out ball, and then seduced. What a tragic tale that would make!

I am in the library writing this. There is a bright fire burning, and I am comfortably ensconced in one of the great leather chairs. There is a writing table, but I prefer to sit here and write. Father is not here—I would not be writing in my diary if he was. He will be back for tea.

I have become quite excited at the thought of writing a novel. It is a pity, though, that I have nothing to practise on. All the people here are quite ordinary, and this house would never do as the setting, it is far too common-place.

I must read something to give me inspiration. Sir Walter Scott, I think, might help to provide a suitably romantic atmosphere. But it is a pity that Father has no really modern works in his library. I wonder if I could persuade him to purchase a copy of one of Miss Brontë's novels. I know they are considered degenerate, but as I have already fallen, and can hardly fall much lower—not here at home, anyway—I might as well enjoy my situation.

February 2nd

I have decided not to attempt a work of fiction. Yesterday, before Father came home, I read some of *Kenilworth*, and it is amazing how reading the work of a great author will persuade one of one's own inability. I will never be able to write a novel. Instead, I will have to content myself with writing reports of the happenings here at home.

Perhaps I will write the story of my coming-out ball after all. I will have to pass the time somehow—it hangs very heavily in the long winter months, especially now that I cannot go about because of my disgrace.

When we had tea in the library yesterday, Father spoke to me about the future. I am not really concerned with the future, but I felt I ought to display some interest, as he was obviously worried. I know, of course, that I will never be able to marry now—not after what has happened. But if marriage is anything like my experience with Charles, I am not sorry. And I will have the baby.

I had never noticed before how Father's hair has gone quite grey in places. I told him not to worry.

"I am perfectly happy," I said. "Really, Father."

He shook his head at that, and would not answer, but his eyes were full of pain. When I tried to impress on him again that I had no feelings at all about my life being ruined (that is what Molly says) he turned away and muttered, "Lizzie should never have gone."

He meant my mother, of course. She died when I was only a few weeks old. I am not supposed to know why, but I persuaded Molly to tell me. It was a complication after child-birth—I don't know the exact details, but she was very delicate, and the birth was too much for her to stand. When she died, Father went wild with grief. Molly was here as nursemaid to me at the time, and she remembers the night my mother died as though it was yesterday. My mother was beautiful. She had very black hair and blue eyes. People used to think she was Irish, but she was really Welsh. She came from a place in Anglesey, and she was the daughter of a gentleman farmer—he hadn't got much money, but my father didn't care that she wasn't an heiress, because he loved her so much.

When they came back after their wedding to live here, I was born the next year. It was a golden day, Molly says, with the sun flurrying and making the trees shine like gold and silver, and the sky was very blue. My father should have been disappointed that

I wasn't a boy, but he wasn't—he was so thrilled that he gave every servant a glass of his best wine to toast me with. He kissed my mother afterwards, but Molly didn't hear what he said to her.

Everyone was happy, but my mother never recovered. She lay in her bed in the big painted bedroom that looks out across the park and the valley, and when I was a few weeks old, she died.

Molly says she wasted away. She says my mother looked like a beautiful ghost lying there with her hair all black as night across the white pillow.

I wonder if I will look like a beautiful ghost when I die. I am not as beautiful as my mother. Her picture is here, in the drawing-room. I would like to have seen her. Sometimes I wonder whether she haunts the house, and I have tried to speak to her, but there is never any answer.

After she died, my father went all stern and grim. He sent the servants away—all except Molly, who had to stay to look after me—and he took to drink. At least, that is what I think he did, but all Molly will say is that he went "very queer". She purses up her mouth when I ask her, and shakes her head.

Later

I am so excited. This afternoon the baby moved. I felt it move, like a butterfly gently moving its wings, trying to get out. It was such a curious feeling, I cried out, and Molly asked what was the matter. When I told her, she looked rather anxious. I think she is afraid I will be delicate like my mother.

I have spent the afternoon waiting to see if it will move again, but it hasn't so far.

I am too excited to write much, but I couldn't wait until tomorrow.

It is still miserable outside. The snow has all gone and the rain has stopped. The wind got up an hour or so ago, but it is warm and cosy here in the library. The fire is bright, and the curtains are drawn and the lamps are lit.

I feel as though a miracle has happened.

February 3rd

I woke this morning to see the sunshine brightening my window. It is a lovely day. The sky deep blue, the sun wintry, but warm. Spring is nearly here, even though the trees are still leafless and the flower-garden bare. I went out after breakfast to look for snowdrops. They are out, scattering the thin grass of the orchard like handfuls of snow. Lovely dainty little things, bravely dancing in the wind.

Doctor Hawk came to see me today. We were expecting him, and I was watching from the White Room for the pony and trap coming along the drive. It came gaily in the sunlight, with the pony stepping high. I could see it flickering in and out of the trees. I told him about the baby moving, and he seemed very pleased. He said he had been waiting for some time for that to happen, but now that it had moved, everything was all right.

I was lying on the *chaise longue* in the drawing-room, and Molly was hovering anxiously on the other side of the room. He asked her to go and fetch a bowl of water, and when she had gone, he turned to me and said he wanted to ask me something. He has got a face like a hawk, lean and rugged, with dark brown side whiskers and moustache. I have known him since I was a little girl.

He asked me whether I am happy here at home.

"Yes, of course," I replied.

He looked puzzled, then asked: "You would not rather go away?"

"Why should I?" I demanded.

He looked even more puzzled, and was just about to speak when Molly came back with the water. After that, he said no more, but he looked at me several times, and after he had had a glass of wine with Father, I heard them in the hall and went out to say goodbye to him.

He had a very curious expression on his face as he turned to me.

"Take good care of yourself, Sophy," he said, and smiled at me. I have the impression that he admires me. Perhaps he thinks I should be prostrated with guilt and shame, but I cannot see what good that would do and it would be most inconvenient, as there would be no one to look after the house.

Father told me at luncheon about his latest discovery on the Dyke. He looked a lot happier after the doctor had gone. He is writing a book about King Offa, who built the Dyke. It runs through our land, about half a mile away from the house. It is a sort of mound, like a long wall of earth, and King Offa built it to keep the English out of Wales, or the Welsh out of England, I forget which.

That is where Father spends most of his time. He has made several interesting discoveries of bones and potsherds, which he keeps in his study. Yesterday, he found what he thinks is a flint axe.

February 4th

We had a merry evening yesterday. Because there was a fire in the drawing-room for Doctor Hawk's visit, I asked Molly to keep it in afterwards, and to open the piano. After supper, I made Father come with me, and he sat by the fire while I played and sang. We were very gay.

I think it would do him good if we could have evenings like that more often. Molly says that after my mother died and

Father sent the servants away, he stopped going out to see people, and he wouldn't receive any callers. We rarely have callers even now—only Doctor Hawk, but I had never really noticed our lack of society until my coming-out ball, when the whole house seemed to leap to life.

It was Doctor Hawk who was responsible for the ball, really. He took Father on one side (Molly told me afterwards) and asked him whether he wanted to see his only daughter growing up a little gypsy, with no companions of her own age or station.

That wasn't fair, of course. Father has taken great pains to see that I have been properly educated, and my lack of friends, as Doctor Hawk calls it, is entirely my own choice. For instance, I was invited to a Christmas party at the Hurst's a few years ago, and Father bought me a new dress and dancing slippers, and even had Miss Angharad from the village come in specially to do my hair—it was most uncomfortable, she twisted it in ringlets and threaded them through with ribbon.

Then Robert took me in the carriage, it was all specially polished and shining for the occasion. I can still remember the excitement of stepping down and going into the house where Mrs Hurst was waiting to receive me. She gave me a hug that nearly broke my bones, and exclaimed over me.

"Why, the little beauty," she said, very loudly, so that everybody heard. "Aren't you a little doll, Miss Roy?"

The house was all sparkly and shining, like a fairy palace, and Mrs Hurst handed me over to her daughters to be taken to see the Christmas Tree. There were lots of other children there, all leaping around and making a great noise, but I was so amazed at the sight of the Christmas Tree that I simply stood still and stared at it. It reached right up to the ceiling, all dark and green with mystery, but with paper chains and candles gleaming among the boughs.

I would have been happy to stare at it all night, I had never seen a Christmas Tree before—but Mrs Hurst's eldest daughter, Paulina, who was wearing a pink muslin frock with her hair in shining fair ringlets, began to tease me. She had a sallow pasty face and horrid pale blue eyes like pebbles. She made fun of my staring at the tree and said rude things about me. I can still remember the uproar after she pinched me, her sharp fingers nipping my arm. I went for her like a fury, and she ran screaming to her Mama, and then I was brought home in disgrace—at least, everyone supposed I was in disgrace, and I heard Mrs Hurst saying loudly: "You were quite right, Harry, we should never have invited that little gypsy, she has no manners at all."

But Robert gave me a wink as he helped me into the carriage, and when I got home and Molly heard all about it, she put witch hazel on my arm where there was quite a nasty bruise, and she sniffed and said that they could say what they liked about my manners, but whoever had done that to me wasn't a lady, not by a long chalk. I said it was Paulina Hurst, who had ringlets and a pink muslin dress, and was very grand, and Molly said: "You can't make a silk purse out of a sow's ear," and made me laugh, and I had bread and milk by the fire in the kitchen and went to bed glad beyond words that I was me.

February 5th

I have been going through the cupboards and chests to find material to make clothes for my baby. I am not very good at sewing, but I will spend a long time over them and do beautiful embroidery. Molly says she will help me.

The baby has moved a few more times, last night and today. I called Molly to put her hand to feel, but she was too late. But she says it doesn't matter—it will get so strong that we will be able to see the movements as the baby kicks. She hugged me when she said that, and shook her head and sniffed very loudly. I thought she was going to cry. But she went to the kitchen instead and prepared a particularly tasty luncheon. I ate two plates of pie. I am sure I will get terribly fat, but as I am never going to get married, and I haven't got to look beautiful, it doesn't matter. Anyway, Molly says I am too skinny and need to build up my strength.

Today is still rather wintry with no sun and the sky dull, but I went out as usual and walked round the garden. The rose bushes look very forlorn. I went down to see the snowdrops again, just to reassure myself that they are still there, and noticed how gnarled and bleak the fruit trees in the orchard are.

Our orchard and gardens are set on a hill that slopes down to the bottom of the park where the well is. They are beautifully laid out, and when Father was a boy they were wonderfully kept, and there used to be lots of gardeners to look after them. But now there is only Robert, and he has to look after the pony and the gardens and lawn and greenhouse and everything.

Doctor Hawk told me that I must rest in the afternoons if I feel tired. I don't feel exactly tired today, but I have come to the library where Molly has made up the fire, and I am sitting here in my favourite leather chair writing this and watching the flames flickering up the wide chimney.

I spend most of my time here in the winter. In the house, there is only Molly, and so, in order to save her work—and also because Father hasn't cared about anything much since my mother died—we don't use all the rooms.

There must have been grand parties here years ago, though, with the ladies in the gowns they used to wear when Father's mother was young—there is a picture of her here, painted at the turn of the century, round about the time Father was born. She was very slim with dark curls clustered round her head in the Greek fashion that was popular, and wearing a thin white dress like a nightgown, with a high waist and showing practically all her shoulders and bosom.

February 6th

Today is Sunday, a miserable and gloomy day, with mist over the garden and the sky so leaden and heavy that Molly has already lit the lamps, although it is not yet four o'clock.

Neither Father nor I have been out. He has spent the day in his study with King Offa, and I have been doing nothing. Perhaps it is because of the weather, or because I have been lazy, but I feel quite out of sorts and I snapped at poor Molly when she came back from chapel. She is very religious on Sundays. I don't know why but that always annoys me, for I think people should be religious all the time or not at all.

Father and I are not religious at all. I think Father was until my mother died. But on the day her coffin was carried out to the hearse, he said that he would never set foot in a church again (he was church, not chapel). Molly told me all about it.

It rained, she said, on the day my mother was buried, and the black plumes on the horses' heads were sodden and my father cried when they carried out the coffin. And when he came back from the funeral, he went out and walked along the Dyke in the rain. It was late, after midnight, when he came back. Molly was lying upstairs waiting to hear him come in.

"Wild, it was, what with the rain on the windows, and the wind howling," she said, when she told me about it. "You were sleeping like a little angel in your cot, I'd left the candle burning and the flame was flickering in the draught, and then I heard his footsteps coming across the yard and I got up to see if he wanted anything—with your mother gone the house was like a tomb, for he'd sent half the servants away the day before. He was wet through, soaked to the skin he was, and his hair all plastered down with rain, dripping wet, leaving soaking puddles behind him on the floor at every step. He looked at me as though he didn't know me—like the devil himself, he was, coming in black like that out of the rain."

It must have been an awful night. Molly never talks of it much, she only told me about it once, and her eyes went dark and round. I don't know if it was then, or before, that Father said he would never set foot in a church again—but he has never been, as long as I can remember, and he has never been to visit my mother's grave.

February 7th

How wrong I was when I said I would never have anything exciting to record in my diary. We have had a great deal of excitement this morning.

To start at the beginning, I was in the yard talking to Robert about the fruit bushes, when we heard a horse arriving. I was so amazed to see who it was—a young man from town, a gentleman, very smart and elegant. At first, I didn't recognise him but when he came forward and bowed, I remembered who he was. His name is Richard Prynne-Edwards. He was at my coming-out ball, and danced with me.

I was furious at being caught unexpectedly with my old gown and cloak on, and my hair bundled up anyhow into a net. Fortunately, Father was in, and it was Father that Mr Prynne-Edwards had come to see. They spent the rest of the morning together in the study. I found out afterwards what they were doing—Father was showing Mr Prynne-Edwards his finds from the Dyke, and telling him all about his research on King Offa. Mr Prynne-Edwards was actually interested. He had come to ask Father whether he would consent to address the Antiquarian Society in town.

Naturally we are all thrilled at the news.

"We have the greatest respect for your father's work, Miss Roy," Mr Prynne-Edwards said to me, as he was about to leave. He bowed over my hand and blushed very red, right up to the roots of his hair, which is fair. I suppose he felt embarrassed at my condition. He has very steady blue eyes, though, and did not look away from me.

The house is in rather a disturbed state as a result of this morning's visit. Father wanted Mr Prynne-Edwards to stay to luncheon, but he couldn't, so Father has taken it on himself to invite Mr Prynne-Edwards to dinner next week. Molly was full of indignation when she heard about it. We have never had a dinner party since I can remember, and she says she doesn't know how she can be expected to manage, with the dining-room in the state it's in, and no warning. I had to calm her down. We can get some of the girls from the cottages to help if necessary, and I will plan a really delicious meal, and get Robert to ransack the greenhouse.

Mr Prynne-Edwards would not come alone—he felt it wouldn't look right, so Father has invited his sister as well. I think she was also at my coming-out ball, but there were so many people, and I cannot remember her.

So you can see that our quiet life is to be stirred up like a pond when a stone falls into it. Already Molly is rushing about muttering under her breath about the work that has got to be done, and Father has gone round with an expression of unearthly bliss on his face since Mr Prynne-Edwards left. He is already sorting his finds and preparing notes for his lecture—for of course, he has accepted the invitation to speak.

I told him he must get a new coat if he is going to do himself justice and not disgrace the name of Roy. He agreed without argument and is intending to go and see his tailor some time this week. The poor man will have a fit—Father has never been near him since my mother died, he has been wearing his old clothes ever since.

I am becoming quite excited. If we are having a dinner party, I must look well too, and apart from my ball gown which I cannot wear for dinner, of course, I have no new clothes either. Like Father, I prefer to be comfortable rather than stylish, and my last dress was made by Miss Gertrude in the village about two years ago. I will have to have a new one.

I think I will spend the evening going through some old copies of *The Englishwoman's Domestic Magazine* to get ideas of the sort of dress I want. My ball gown was deep red—everybody was very shocked by it, they thought I should have had white—but for my new dinner dress, I think I will have green. Green velvet, perhaps (the dining-room can be draughty).

Molly and I will go to town and buy the material tomorrow. I have quite decided. What a flurry! But I must admit, I like it. It is like being rushed along on a railway train. I have never been on one, but I have heard how fast they go.

February 8th

We have been to town this morning. We were there until now; the carriage has just come back and Molly and I have unpacked our parcels. Father has gone into his study, and Molly is making the tea. I have come here to the White Room—the library is chilly because the fire had gone out.

The White Room is the place I come to when I want to be really alone—not like the library, where I feel surrounded by friends. I like to be able to think sometimes, and this is a very good place for thinking. It is on the other side of the house, away from the kitchen and furthest from the yard, so it is very quiet with the garden and lawn below the windows and all the soft white light full of flickerings and shadows.

I have chosen the material for my dress. We saw a lovely green—a sort of deep moss colour—and it is to be made on the severe lines that suit me.

We have had a glorious spending spree. Father was like a child. I have never known him spend money like this before, but he has not only ordered two new coats from the tailor, he has also bought one ready-made for the dinner party, because the others will not be ready in time. He bought some trousers and new shirts—the old ones are threadbare in places—and gloves, and a fine black hat and new boots.

I had a new bonnet and coat, and some silk to make up—I couldn't resist the colour, it is amber, a clear glowing amber, and we bought some deep brown velvet ribbon to trim it with. I have also had new gloves and boots, and some beautiful underclothes. Molly and Robert were not forgotten either. Molly is singing in the kitchen, I'm sure. She is now the proud possessor of a velvet and gold beaded purse from Paris. It was wrapped up in soft paper that smells of violets, and Molly was so thrilled that I thought she would either explode or kiss Father there and then in the Emporium. Robert has had a new hat and whip and some high boots for when he drives us in the carriage.

It made me laugh. All the grand ladies and gentlemen in town looked down their noses at us, and the poorer people and tradesmen must have thought we were penniless, the carriage is so old and shabby. But then someone recognised Father, and everyone whispered. When we went into the Emporium, Father walked like a king with his head in the air, and the clerks and assistants all bowed—they couldn't help themselves. It was "Yes, Sir John" and "No, Sir John" all day.

I asked Father, when he took us to luncheon at the George, whether we could really afford all this finery—we have also ordered new table linen and new curtains for the dining room, of heavy dark red brocade. He looked at me, and his eyes flashed.

"Don't talk nonsense, Sophy," he said.

But I suppose things must be all right. After all, we have hardly spent any money since I was a baby—except for my coming-out ball—so Father must be quite wealthy. The estate has been doing well, as far as I know. We do not hear much about it, of course, for Father lets Mr Turner and his business partners run it almost entirely. There was some talk before my coming-out ball about my dowry—Doctor Hawk, who tried very hard to get Father to do things in what he called "the right way" for me, said it must be settled (Molly was listening to all this, and it was the day when Doctor Hawk asked Father if he wanted me to grow up a gypsy with no prospects or friends of my own station). I don't think Father ever said what my dowry was going to be, though, and Doctor Hawk realised he was fighting a losing battle, but he did manage to persuade Father to hold a ball for me. It was only afterwards, when I came back, and sent for him to tell him I thought I was going to have a baby, that he admitted that perhaps he might have been wrong.

"My dear child," he said—he had gone quite white. "My dear Sophy—you can't mean this—this dreadful thing."

"I do, and it's not dreadful," I said. I was a bit impatient.

He could hardly speak. He took my hand, and looked quite agonised. "What have we done to you?" he said, shaking his head. "Between us, we've ruined every chance you might have had of a happy life."

I told him that was silly. "I'm perfectly happy," I said. "Except that I feel sorry for Charles' wife—poor thing. He must have hurt her terribly."

Doctor Hawk was gaping at me by this time. He sat for a few moments looking so stunned that I thought he was feeling ill. After that, he spoke to me quite seriously—as though I was grown up, as old as he is. He said he thought Father might have been right about not having a ball.

"I feel as though I have trapped a linnet, and put it in a cage," he said, shaking his head.

He asked whether I would like him to break the news to Father, but I told him I had already told Father about it.

"And how did your father take it?" he said, looking very worried.

"He went out to the Dyke and dug for a whole day without coming in for luncheon," I answered. "But he is all right now."

Doctor Hawk looked at a loss for words. He said he would come back and see me again, and bring me a tonic, and he drove away looking like a sleepwalker.

I hear Molly calling me. Tea is ready. The light is getting dim here, but I hadn't noticed. The library fire will be blazing merrily now. I can hear Father's footsteps crossing the hall. After tea, I will parade in my new bonnet and coat, like a fine lady of fashion.

February 9th

Such a commotion was never heard since last year, when we were getting ready for the ball. I have been reminded of it, feeling the house coming to life around me, even though the circumstances are very different. The piano-tuner has been this morning, and some people came from the upholsterer's to see about having the chairs re-covered. Molly has got Mair, from the cottages, with her in the kitchen, both polishing away at the silver for dear life.

I have been busy this morning, and I feel a little tired this afternoon and in need of solitude again, so I have come to the White Room. It is strange how this room draws me. Nobody else comes here, apart from Molly, who occasionally dusts and polishes. But the room is never used—it had not been used for years until Father opened it up for my coming-out ball.

The ball was a great occasion in our lives, of course. Miss Jones was still with us when Father broke the news that he was giving a ball for me. She went white, then red, I remember, and immediately started chattering about gowns and jewels. She was to come, naturally, because even though she had been my governess and was then a sort of companion, it would have been very hard to leave her out, and let her go to sleep upstairs listening to the violins and the laughter.

We had a small orchestra—it was on a raised platform at one end of the room, over in the corner. The floor had been polished, and the room was decorated with festoons of greenery and flowers. Oh, the flowers! The scent was overwhelming, it drifted through the whole house. We had an army of maids and footmen who came from town for the occasion, and the buffet was laid out in the parlour just off the Dome Room.

Miss Jones and I had spent the whole afternoon helping with the arrangements—all sorts of things kept happening. One of the girls who came to help was sick, and had to be taken home, and somebody upset one of the vases, and one of the farm cats got into the larder—Molly nearly had fits. We didn't have time to start our own preparations until quite late in the afternoon. Miss Jones wore a dreadfully fussy dress in maroon velvet.

"I think it makes me look—well, quite regal, don't you, Sophy dear?" she said, when she came to show me. I didn't have the heart to spoil her pleasure. Miss Angharad came to do my hair, and I let her do Miss Jones's as well. She had it piled up in very elaborate curls—it was a copy of something she had seen in a French fashion magazine, but it didn't suit her at all. Poor Miss Jones!

As for my dress, Miss Jones had tried to persuade me to have a dress of white muslin, embroidered with silver. She said it would make me look like an angel. I said I thought it would look as though I was wearing a shroud. I chose red, and had a crinoline petticoat for the very first time. I had to practise walking about in it. It felt quite strange, but terribly grown-up. I can smile now—I am smiling, this minute, as I write. As though putting your hair up and wearing a crinoline could make you any older than you are.

February 10th

I went out this morning to walk, and decided to go as far as the end of the drive. It was exhilarating walking along the ridge, with the cold air blustering at my skirt and nipping my face and fingers. The poplars were moving in the wind, but stiffly, as though they were so cold they could not bend. They looked like witches' besoms against the sky. I reached the gate, where the drive opens onto the road, and I was standing getting my breath, and looking down over the park and the valley, when I heard a horse coming along the road. It came round the corner, and I thought I must be seeing things—the rider was Charles.

I think he was as surprised to see me as I was to see him. I have not set eyes on him since the day when Father came to fetch me home.

I didn't know what to say. I felt dismayed, for some inexplicable reason—not because of my condition, as under my cloak, that hardly shows, but because I didn't want to speak to him in case I said things I might regret. I was hurt, too—and angry. It was wicked and cruel of him to come here, after what happened.

As soon as I saw him, I turned and started to walk back along the drive, but he called me.

"Sophy! Miss—Roy!"

I had to turn. He had dismounted. I went back.

"I was just passing—didn't think I'd see anybody," he started to explain incoherently. "Just wanted to see the house—"

He took my hands in his impetuous way, before I could stop him.

"Oh Sophy, you're more beautiful than ever," he said. "I never would have thought you could look more lovely than that night when I danced with you at the ball, but your cheeks are like holly berries, you look like a goddess of the wild—a Dryad!"

His voice had the deep music in it that I have tried hard to forget.

"You must not say these things, Mr Beaumont," I tried to say, "Please go away."

He protested that he meant it all, that he hadn't been able to get me out of his thoughts, and at this deceitfulness, I could not help it, I lost my temper. I pulled myself away and told him that I despised him, and never wanted to see him again. He was taken aback. He stood there with his mouth open, looking like a fish. He is really very handsome, but I steeled myself against looking at him. It hurt to look at his face and remember how he had betrayed me.

"You don't understand, Sophy, I'm in torment," he said. "I still love you—and you loved me too—once," he added rather threateningly.

Well, I was so shaken with fury at this that I said the first thing that came into my head.

"I thought so at the time—but now I can see it would be impossible ever to love somebody like you. Goodbye, Mr Beaumont," I said in a hard, cold voice, and glared at him.

He looked at me for a moment in a hurt, unbelieving way, as though he was a dog, and I had whipped him. But I carried on glaring quite haughtily, and in the end, he turned away and mounted and rode off.

I felt both sad and glad at the same time to see him go.

February 11th

I have been reading what I wrote yesterday about Charles. What a silly ending to the grand affair that had all the county gossiping. I wonder if things are always like that, and that only in novels does everything end smoothly. Life is very unsatisfactory, really. It all seems to be made up of bits and pieces, and things never work as one would expect them. I tried to explain this to Molly this morning when I was in the kitchen, but she didn't understand what I meant. I heard her saying to Mair as I came out: "Poor lamb! She gets these fancies with her in her condition."

I wonder if Mr Prynne-Edwards would understand what I meant. The truth was just what I told Charles yesterday—and I hope it has taught him a lesson. Now that I know what he is really like, I would never be able to love anybody so shallow and worthless. He is handsome and wealthy enough—his family lives at Pengwern Hall, which is nearly as old as this house, and much more fashionably kept—and he was married last year to one of the Hurst daughters. The middle one. Her name is Christina, and she is just like her horrid sister Paulina who pinched me at the Christmas party, with a nasty whining voice and eyes like flints.

But he had no right to tell me he loved me—it was unforgivable—and he deserved to be taught a lesson. This is what I mean about life being curious. It ought to have been me who was left broken-hearted and pining with grief and shame, but I am really much wiser for the experience, and I will soon have the baby to play with—how it will brighten Molly's life, and Father's too, especially if it is a boy. I can see Father getting out the old archery butts from the room over the stables and setting them up on the lawn, and teaching his grandson how to draw a bow.

How dismal the weather is. I can hardly see to write, and the rain is pouring down outside the windows. The garden is a quagmire and the terrace was streaming this morning when I went to the White Room to look out.

Later

This miserable day has become one of delight for me. A messenger came splashing up the drive this afternoon with a parcel for Father, and he came into the library with a twinkle in his eye that I have rarely seen before, and held out the parcel to me.

I opened it. Three volumes of a book called *Jane Eyre*, by Currer Bell, that is, Miss Brontë. I was so delighted, I sprang up and hugged Father. He was pleased at my response, and he went back to the study looking cheerful. He says he has also ordered some other works by the Brontës (apparently there are three of them—they were three sisters, but two of them are dead now) but I am quite happy with my prize of this afternoon. I can't make up my mind whether to start reading it now or wait until after tea. I have an hour before tea—I will begin *Jane Eyre*.

February 12th

The rain has cleared today, it is a cold gloomy day but I have been warm by the library fire deep in the adventures of Jane. I forgot about everything—Molly had to come and fetch me when I didn't answer her call for luncheon, and I could hardly wait to get back to Thornfield Hall.

It is such an exciting book, and so real. I have not finished it yet, but already I know that I will never forget Jane and her awful childhood at Lowood School—it made me realize how lucky I was in my own childhood. Molly is very fond of saying "Count Your Blessings" but I had not realized I had so many.

The only thing I don't agree with is Jane's refusal to stay with Mr Rochester after she found out about his mad wife. It seems cruel to have left him for something that was not his fault, and he would have needed her more than ever. In fact, I think she should have counted her blessings in having been loved by such a man as Mr Rochester. I wonder if I could love somebody like that, stern and dark, and violent. I spent a pleasant half hour last night before I went to sleep pondering on the question, and I have decided that I might love him if he had real worth. But I have never met anybody like that. I wonder whether Miss Brontë has? I picture her as a person very like Jane, slim and upright with very dark smooth hair and clear eyes.

Because of my reading, I have neglected my duties today. Molly has been tut-tutting and shaking her head. But I will see to things tomorrow or on Monday, that will be plenty of time, and everything is going quite smoothly.

The dining-room is already transformed for our dinner party, with the new curtains hung. Molly and Mair, who seem to like it with us, have given the rooms a good clean, from ceiling to floor, and everything is sparkling. The new curtains look very elegant, the lamps are all trimmed and ready to be lit. We have candles on the table in the silver holders from my mother's old room—they were quite black, and Molly spent hours polishing them. The sideboard is dark oak, not modern, but it has been polished up with oil and vinegar, and beeswax and shines like an ebony sun. The rugs have been thoroughly shaken, and the floor polished.

I have chosen the menu. We are to have soup, an entree of fish, saddle of lamb, syllabub and then coffee and some of Father's best brandy (actually his father was responsible for the cellar—Father has never been very interested in drinking since he took up antiquities). Molly pickled our crop of walnuts from the great walnut tree in the park, last year—they are delicious and we will have them after the dessert. It will be quite a simple meal, but I feel most strongly that we should not make an exhibition of ourselves. I don't want Mr Prynne-Edwards and his sister to laugh at us.

He was very pleasant at the ball. I have remembered more about him. When we danced, he told me, very stiffly, that he liked my dress.

"It puts these pinks and blues to shame, Miss Roy," he said, and added in a low voice: "It makes you look like—like a deep, glowing red carnation in the middle of a group of sweetpeas."

What a funny thing for him to have said. I wonder if he is interested in flowers? I will ask Father to make sure we have some red carnations for the night of the dinner party.

I think I was not paying much attention to him at the ball, because Charles had already asked me to go away with him that night and was looking at me across the room while I danced with Mr Prynne-Edwards. I remember that when I went out of the White Room to get my cloak and change my dress before slipping away with Charles, I was in such a hurry that I forgot my fan, and I caught sight of Mr Prynne-Edwards coming across with his eyes on me, and looking very concerned. I stopped in the doorway, and he bowed and said:

"You left your fan, Miss Roy."

I thanked him, and he looked at me as though he was going to say something else, then he shut his mouth very firmly and bowed again and I came out into the hall, and then my memory is confused. I remember the single candle lit in my bedroom as I hastily took off my ball gown and put on my old green walking-dress, and cloak and bonnet, and my reflection in the mirror looking at me with bright eyes and flushed cheeks. It was an adventure and I enjoyed it all—except for my discovery later that Charles was merely amusing himself with me and that he didn't love me at all. I was beginning to get very tired of his company by the time Father caught up with us.

February 13th

A beautiful sunny day—a great contrast to last week's gloomy Sunday. The sun is pure gold, but not warm. Outside, the cold air soon nips fingers and toes if one stands still. I have been out, down to the orchard and to see if the crocuses are out—they are not. It is so clear today that I could see right across the park, and down into the valley. The church tower is visible, among the trees and roofs of the town—all the fashionable ladies and gentlemen will be getting out of their carriages in their Sunday best dresses and bonnets and coats, and rustling into the church and up the aisles.

I wonder if Mr Prynne-Edwards has gone to church. I expect so. He is the sort of person who would be very particular about going to church on Sundays, or so I imagine.

I have finished reading *Jane Eyre*, I was so glad it ended happily. I should have loved Mr Rochester, too, even blind and mutilated, and even if his wife had still lived. Why are there no such men in this part of the country? I suppose they must all live in Yorkshire—but it would be exciting to meet one.

Molly is laying the table in the dining-room for our luncheon. There is a delicious smell of roast beef coming from the kitchen—I am becoming more and more hungry these days. Doctor Hawk seemed to think I might be likely to lose my appetite, but there's no chance of that, I feel better than ever, and my hair and skin seem to glow. Molly commented on it the other day, I heard her saying to Mair—who is naturally avid for gossip about us—as I was coming out of the kitchen, "Born to have babies, you'd swear it, and her without even a ring, poor soul."

Sometimes I think Molly dramatises things too much!

February 14th

Something so delightful has happened today, I must write about it. I have had a Valentine! I have never had one in my life before, and I have no idea who this one is from. It really is a mystery. At first, when I opened it, I thought it must be a mistake, but my name was on it, written very clearly.

Who can have sent it? Molly and Mair exclaimed over it in the kitchen—it is really lovely, with exquisitely-painted red roses, and it says "The roses speak for me"—they were quite thrilled, but mystified, the same as me. It's the most romantic thing that has happened since my ball.

Mair's eyes went even wider than usual when I showed it to them.

"Oh, miss, you must have got a secret admirer," she exclaimed, clasping her hands.

Molly looked very suspicious, but I could tell even she was puzzled. I have no idea at all who the sender could be—unless it's Charles, but after seeing his face when he rode off, I don't think Charles would bother to send me a Valentine.

I did wonder—but secretly, only to myself, whether it could

have been Mr Prynne-Edwards. But I must stop being ridiculous. He is a very respectable young man, and even if he admires me—and why should I imagine he admires me!—my condition would discourage him. But somebody must have sent it.

We have spent the afternoon speculating most enjoyably. I showed Father the Valentine, and he looked quite pleased.

"Who sent it, eh?" he asked, and I had to admit I didn't know. He laughed, one of his quick barks of laughter, and then he said: "Your mother would have been proud of you, Sophy."

He has never mentioned my mother for a long time—not like that. I went all warm with a sort of tingly blush, and said: "Would she, Father?"

He laughed again and said: "Yes, Lizzie would have been proud of you—but you'd have frightened her out of her wits."

I wonder what he meant. He went back to his study still laughing, and I came into the kitchen to get Molly to wash my hair. I must have it ready for the dinner party, and it needs a few days before it will settle down and be coaxed tidily into place. Normally I bundle it into a net, but I am going to get Miss Angharad to do it in the very latest style, with little ringlets round my face. On second thoughts, though, I don't think they would suit me. I shall be very severe, with my hair swept back and twisted into a knot with French flowers decorating it—just one or two. We bought them when we were in town.

I am going to wear my dark red shawl over my dress. It will keep off the draughts and also hide my figure. I have no jewellery, but I don't think that matters, the dress and my new kid shoes will be elegant enough.

I am sitting in the kitchen writing this. Molly is sitting opposite me. My hair is drying round my shoulders. She is sewing, and she knows I am writing in my diary, but although she is curious, she is quite approving—in the awful books that Molly reads (when she reads at all) the heroine always keeps a secret diary where she records what happens to her.

Molly has just asked me what I can find to write about. I told her I am writing about what we have been doing today, and the preparations for the dinner party. She didn't seem convinced. I am sure she thinks I lead a secret life—What a delightful idea! Imagine me—with my figure quite going by now, flitting off to meet a tall dark gentleman by moonlight. I must write a second diary, simply to keep Molly happy. I will put the most outrageous things in it.

I have just had an idea! Could Doctor Hawk have sent my Valentine?

February 15th

I had to break off yesterday because Robert came in to sit by the fire. He was rather tongue-tied when he saw I was there—I don't often sit in the kitchen since I grew out of being a child. Miss Jones never approved anyway. But I put away my diary, and Molly and Robert and I got quite merry, we talked and sang and played word-games, and then I had steaming bread-and-milk, as I used to when I was a little girl.

This morning is blustery and rainy, and raw. I have been out to walk in the garden and orchard, well wrapped up. The snowdrops are still in the orchard, trembling in the grass as the wind pulls at them. You would never imagine that such fragile things could survive.

There is no sign of the crocuses blooming yet. They are coming up, but are still green and secretive. The daffodils are a few inches above the earth, like green spears.

In the old days when my father was a little boy, there used to be lots of horses in the stables and the family used to go riding in the park. I have never had a horse to ride. We have the pony, and when we go out in the carriage, we use the horses from the farm. But neither Father nor I are interested in hunting—I am sure it would make me sick to see a kill—and I do not really like riding.

In any case, we do not go out much. We are a very closely knit family here. My father's mother and father were killed in a terrible tragic accident, long before I was born. They were together in a curricle which grandfather was driving himself, when it over-turned and they were both killed. He must have been going at a furious pace. I think he was a bit of a rake, and my grandmother (the one in the portrait in the white dress and curls) was just as high-spirited. She was a beauty, so I have been told, but she had the most terrible temper—I expect they suited each other, because my grandfather was the same.

On my mother's side, there are no relations either—both my mother and father were only children. My mother's parents are still alive, I think, but they live in some remote part of Anglesey, and after my mother died Father never went to see them.

So we do not go out very often. Miss Jones was always bemoaning the loneliness of her life while she was here—I think the real trouble was that she was looking for a husband, and there was nobody handsome and wealthy enough to suit her tastes. Molly used to say that Miss Jones was chasing after Father.

"Disgusting it was," she said, afterwards, with a sniff. "A real harpy she was—set her cap at him right from the start, I could see that."

Of course, Father wasn't the least bit interested—as though he could ever have looked at Miss Jones after my mother, with her lovely dark hair and delicate face and huge dark eyes. I suppose if he had been a different sort of man he might have philandered with her, but being Father, he never even noticed she was there, he was far too interested in King Offa and the Dyke.

I have just thought of something else to keep me occupied, as well as writing in my diary. I will write a history of the house. It is very old—part of it was built in the reign of Queen Elizabeth, and lots of thrilling things must have happened here. It would please Father if I showed an interest in history too, even though this house does not go back as far as King Offa. There must be lots of old books and histories here—I will ask him about it at luncheon. It is nearly ready.

February 16th

Our dinner party is tomorrow. We have half-forgotten about it during the week, or at least I have. Today we have been making our final preparations. Now everything is ready. The table in the dining room is polished, the room itself shining with scrubbing and washing, the new curtains hanging. The table linen is ready, the silver polished, the flowers ordered and tomorrow the butcher will be delivering our meat and the fishmonger will be bringing the fish.

Now that I have bustled about to Molly's satisfaction, I have come into the library for a rest. There are two girls with her in the kitchen, Mair and Shan, who have both been fitted out with white caps and aprons, and Molly is teaching them how to wait on the gentry. They are both bright-eyed, cheerful little things, the kitchen seems more lively for having them around. I wonder if I can persuade Father that we really need two new maids.

Yesterday, I asked him about the history books and told him I was going to investigate the history of the house. He asked whether I was thinking of turning into a blue-stocking, but he seemed quite pleased and even let me have a private diary that has always been kept in his study. It belonged to his great-grandmother, on his father's side. She lived early in the last century, here, in the house.

I spent the afternoon reading it. It is quite fascinating really, I would never have suspected, but she was a supporter of the Jacobites. She wrote letters to Prince James Edward, and she made her husband (my great-great-grandfather) go to the meetings of the Jacobite society in town. It was called the Circle of the White Rose, and all the gentlemen used to drink to the King over water and break their glasses.

My great-great-grandfather sounds a bit like Charles, except that his wife used to order him around far more than Charles' wife orders him. I cannot imagine Christina Hurst ever giving an order to anybody, not even the horde of servants at Pengwern Hall. She does nothing but whine and cry. No wonder that Charles wanted to get away from her, but that was his own fault really, because if he does not love her, he should never have married her.

I expect his father, Sir Ifor, told him to. Sir Ifor has a purple face and wears the most unsuitable colours. He looks dreadful in the hunting pink, but he spends most of his time hunting. He once pinched my bottom when I was at Pengwern Hall, a long time ago, when I went there with Miss Jones to take tea with Lady Megan, and I slapped his face and Miss Jones fainted and Lady Megan started to cry, and Sir Ifor blinked and then said: "Damned spirited little filly." It was the last time I ever went to Pengwern Hall. I wonder if Sir Ifor has ever pinched Christina Hurst's bottom.

It is amazing that Charles is so handsome, because Sir Ifor is so ugly (although he must have been handsome before he became so fat) and Lady Megan is terribly thin and washed out—I expect that is because she is always crying. They were all at my ball. Lady Megan wore violet silk, with an enormous crinoline, and she was absolutely dripping with diamonds—far too many for good taste—and Sir Ifor started demanding where the punch bowl was, practically as soon as they arrived.

I think I liked the house best before the guests arrived. I came down in my red dress, all ready, with my hair in the curls on each side of my head, shivering because the shoulders of the dress were so low, and with my silk petticoats rustling. I can remember coming down the stairs from my bedroom, and just at that moment, the hall was empty, and I felt strange, like a ghost of a lady from long ago, in an unfamiliar dress, sweeping down the stairs (at least, as well as I could, because the staircase is quite narrow).

Then I heard all the noises, one by one, the fiddlers tuning up and the maids and footmen quarrelling in the kitchen and people getting ready to receive the guests in the Dome Room. The candles were ablaze everywhere, and the house was full of light and the scent of flowers.

Then Father came out from the White Room, very tall and distinguished in his evening dress, with the white shirt very crisp, and he took my hand and looked at me, from the top of my head to the soles of my red dancing slippers that matched the dress.

"Sophy," he said, as though there was something in his throat that was stopping him from speaking properly. "My little Sophy."

Then he kissed my hand lightly over the cream kid glove and then the first carriage rolled up the drive, and the guests began to arrive.

February 17th

They are to come at eight. We have been very busy all day, and I am just having a rest before the excitement of the evening. I am in the library—this has escaped the scrubbing and polishing and is its old familiar self with the big shabby chairs and writing desk sitting quietly around me like old friends.

I have not started work on my history of the house yet, because we have been too preoccupied with the dinner party today. I have been helping Molly with the cooking, and the kitchen is full of savoury smells. I am hungry already. We are not accustomed to such a large dinner in the evening, so in order for us to have some appetite left, Father and I only had a very light tea, some bread and butter and some of Molly's ginger preserve that she made last year.

My dress is all ready, it came yesterday, and Molly has laid it out upstairs on my bed, with my new kid shoes and red shawl, and Miss Angharad is coming at any moment—Robert has gone to fetch her—with her combs and curling tongs, ready to do my hair. I think she had better do it in here, by the fire. I know there is no mirror, and it is unheard of for a lady to finish her toilette in the library, but it is so cold upstairs and nobody will see.

I hoped it might have been a pleasant day today, but it is cold, grey and raw. I think I almost prefer the snow to this rawness, it creeps into the house, and if it lasts much longer I am sure we will all have bad chests.

I can hear a noise in the hall. Misss Angharad has arrived, so I must go to see to my toilette.

Later

I am wandering about with nothing to do for the moment. I am dressed and ready, my hair is done, but the guests have not yet arrived. My green dress looks quite charming, I think. It makes my skin look fairer and my hair blacker, and I was also pleased to find I looked quite slender. Miss Angharad, who twitters like a sparrow, was scandalised that I was not going to lace tightly, but I refused absolutely, as I am sure tight lacing would harm the baby.

I think Miss Angharad felt she should have been shocked by my condition, but she is so curious that she did not bother to faint in case she missed anything interesting. She is a dear really, she has bright little eyes, just like a bird, and a head that she is always putting on one side. She stores up pieces of gossip like crumbs, and I am certain that everybody in the village will have heard before long about our dinner party and my dress and the way I did my hair.

She has done it beautifully, swept back in a smooth curve from my face, and secured into a knot, with the French flowers in it, at the nape of my neck.

She told me I looked very elegant when everything was finished, and I paraded before her in my dress and shawl.

Oh! Voices! Our guests are here. I must go.

PART TWO

February 19th

I was too depressed yesterday to write anything in my diary. It was a raw and bitter morning, and the house was full of echoes of our dinner party—it really was awful. The whole thing was a mistake. I was sorry that we had looked forward to it so much, for our disappointment was all the greater when it turned into a dreadful debacle. All yesterday I felt dreadfully ashamed of myself. I am afraid I behaved very badly.

I really must be feeling low, for me to admit defeat. Nonsense, Sophy! It was not our fault at all, everything would have been perfect if Miss Prynne-Edwards had not come.

To start at the beginning—they arrived in style, and Father and I stood in the hall to receive them. Mr Prynne-Edwards was his usual serious self. He looked very distinguished in his dinner jacket, it showed up the fairness of his hair and the blueness of his eyes.

Miss Prynne-Edwards is just like a doll, a lovely French doll with a painted waxen face and frail porcelain shoulders. She was wearing yellow, with flounces of lace, and as soon as she came in, the hall was full of the scent of lemon verbena. She had a fur-trimmed cloak and muff and a fur-trimmed hood over her yellow hair. Father and I stared, taken aback with admiration, as Mr Prynne-Edwards introduced us. Her name is Clarissa.

We started off the evening well enough. We went in for dinner, and Miss Prynne-Edwards hung on Father's arm delightfully and said her brother had told her such a lot about him, and Father looked startled and barked: "Has he, hah?"

"Oh yes," she said, fluttering her eyelashes and dimpling.

I was a bit apprehensive because I thought she was teasing Father and he did not realize it—he is very sensitive and would be hurt if he thought a young lady of fashion was laughing at him behind his back. Mr Prynne-Edwards thought the same, I know, because he hung back as they went in, and whispered to me, in an embarrassed fashion, "Miss Roy—I must apologize—"

"For what, Mr Prynne-Edwards?" I asked in some surprise.

"I don't know, yet," he said, looking very grim and anxious. "But Clarissa is in one of her moods. I thought it would be a good idea for her to come and meet you, but I am beginning to feel that—well, I might have made a mistake."

This conversation rather amazed me, as you might well imagine, but as dinner progressed, I began to understand what he meant. Miss Prynne-Edwards praised everything so extravagantly that it was quite embarrassing. She declared that the soup was superb, and the fish delightful, and she flirted outrageously with Father, flattering him and pretending to take an interest in King Offa, and all the time, I am sure she was laughing behind her eyes. Mr Prynne-Edwards looked quite agonized, he hid his face over his plate and wouldn't meet my gaze.

And then, when poor Mair, who was sweating with nervousness, let a dish drop and it broke on the floor, and she burst into tears, Miss Prynne-Edwards gave up all pretence and absolutely shook with laughter, and I could imagine how she would tell the story of our disastrous evening at all the fashionable dinner parties in town, and make fun of Father, and I began to feel so furiously angry that I did a terrible thing.

When we had finished dinner, and left Father and Mr Prynne-Edwards sitting uncomfortably over their port, I asked Miss Prynne-Edwards if she would like to see the haunted room where one of the servant girls is said to have hanged herself a long time ago, and I spun such a tale (Miss Jones' library books from the circulating library in town came in very useful), that I need not tell you what happened when I took her up to the attics with a candle.

She screamed so loudly that everybody including Molly and the girls came running, and the coachman who had brought them in the carriage. She tore her yellow dinner dress and covered it with dust and cobwebs by catching her foot and falling in the top corridor when the candle went out, and then she got hysterical and I had to send Molly to fetch my smelling salts which I never use, and Father carried her downstairs in his arms, and put her on the sofa in the drawing room. She cried that she wouldn't stay in the house a minute longer, and insisted on going home, so Mr Prynne-Edwards took her home in their carriage, wrapped in her fur-trimmed cloak and hood, leaning against him as though she was ill. He looked very white and tight-lipped, and never spoke a word except to bow very correctly and say goodbye.

I felt dreadful afterwards, when they had gone. I shouldn't have frightened her! Mr Prynne-Edwards will never forgive me—oh dear! He will never come here again.

Oh, well! *Kismet*, as they say in the east. I am very philosophical.

February 20th

We talked about the dinner party at tea yesterday, and Father admitted—or rather, he told me without any prompting—that he considered Miss Prynne-Edwards a frivolous fashion-plate, the sort of female he really abhors.

"She's learnt her lesson, though, I'll wager," he barked, giving me a very dry look. "She'll not be in a hurry to cross swords with the Roys again."

I have been amusing myself today, after the chores were done, by beginning my history of the house. I have done some investigating, and when I went out this morning, I went round to the chapel to read the date over the door, which I had forgotten about. The chapel is really part of the house. It is a private chapel built for the use of the family living here, when the house was first built.

Really it is a most interesting building, very small—there is only room for about half a dozen people inside—and built of grey stone blocks, the same as the house, with a gabled front surmounted by stone balls. It has one tiny window, that looks out over the garden, and there is very little light inside.

We keep it locked up now—Father has got the key in his study. I wonder whether anyone has ever used it since it was built—perhaps my great-great-grandmother, the one who was a Jacobite, used to have Mass celebrated there secretly—she was a Roman Catholic, of course. I know that from her diary, but I am sure she only became a Roman Catholic because the rest of the family were Church of England. If she was alive today, I expect she would be doing someting like going out to Scutari with Miss Nightingale—or perhaps she might even be fighting alongside the soldiers.

I have a piece of paper in front of me with the date of the chapel on it (1589) and I have taken several local histories from the shelves and am going to potter through them to see if there is any mention of who built the house—I think it was a family called Kyffin. The Roys married the Kyffin heiress in the time of Charles II.

February 21st

I found some primulas this morning, yellow ones, blooming bravely among their green leaves in the garden. The weather is still cold and chill, there is hardly any colour at all in the view over the valley, and for the last two or three days there has been a powdering of white on the hills beyond our ridge.

But I feel that spring is on the way at last. I woke this morning feeling so cheerful and gay that I got up before Molly had brought me any hot water. She was still doing the fires downstairs when I went down, and was amazed to see me, but I helped her with the fires—although she would not let me carry any coal—and then we had breakfast together in the kitchen, with steaming tea out of the old blue, lustre mugs that stand in rows on the dresser. I told Molly that I wanted to start getting a room ready for the baby. Her face lit up, and I could tell she thoroughly approved.

I can hear voices in the hall. What can have happened? Surely we have not got a visitor—and it's not Doctor Hawk's day to come.

Later

It was Mr Prynne-Edwards. I almost fell over with surprise when I saw him, because I was certain he would never set foot in the house again. He has brought me a present—oh, such a lovely delightful little thing, even though Molly has prophesied dire calamities and sworn that she won't have the little brute in her clean kitchen, she has already made him up a bed in the corner, with a tray of earth to teach him to be clean in the house.

To start at the beginning, I went out into the hall, and there was Mr Prynne-Edwards, looking very red but determined and carrying a basket. I was glad that he had not caught me unawares this time; I had done my hair tidily this morning, and because I felt cheerful I had put on a dress of red plaid trimmed with green, it is quite flattering, even though it is old.

I told Mr Prynne-Edwards that Father was out on the Dyke, and he went redder and said, very stiffly: "It's not your father—I hoped to see you, Miss Roy. I would like you to accept this—in grateful thanks for your hospitality—the other evening."

Well, I could tell there was something alive in the basket, so I opened it, hoping it wouldn't be something outlandish. And inside, was the sweetest little puppy, sitting shivering on a warm cushion. I lifted him out, exclaiming with delight.

"I have never had a puppy," I said to Mr Prynne-Edwards, and he looked quite gratified and told me the little thing is a real thoroughbred with a long pedigree. He comes from a famous kennel in town, he is a retriever, but I am going to keep him as a household pet. I have decided to call him Mr Rochester—after Miss Brontë's hero, although at the moment he looks more like a scrap of crumpled velvet than a hero.

Mr Prynne-Edwards did not stay for very long. I asked him to stay for tea, because I knew Father would be in for tea, and Father has just found a Neolithic tool of some sort on the Dyke, which he has been very anxious to show Mr Prynne-Edwards. But he said he was sorry, he could not stay for tea. He did, however, accept a glass of wine, and sat with me in the library (there is no fire in the drawing room) for half an hour or so.

I asked after Miss Prynne-Edwards and said I was sorry about her fright on the night of the dinner party, and Mr Prynne-Edwards looked rather strained and said: "I wanted to—apologize for her, Miss Roy."

He said that their father is away in the Midlands a lot on business connected with the iron works (the Prynne-Edwards' are iron masters) and their mother is an invalid and spends all her time lying on a *chaise longue*, and that as a result: "I think Clarissa has been given too much headway, Miss Roy. The servants will do anything for her, and she—well, has never had any discipline and everyone has petted and spoiled her until her head is quite turned."

I wondered why he was telling me all this, but said politely that I quite understood, and I was sorry I had not behaved better myself.

Then he actually smiled—he looks very attractive when he smiles—and said he thought the experience had been quite good for her. And then, without any more ado, he got up to go, and has gone, leaving me rather bewildered.

February 22nd

Doctor Hawk came to see me this morning. He seemed quite pleased with my progress. He asked me how I had been feeling, and I told him, very well, with no signs of faintness or sickness.

"Motherhood suits you, Sophy, I'm bound to admit," he said, smiling. "I have never seen you look so blooming. Why, you're positively radiant, child."

Well, I decided there and then that it must have been Doctor Hawk who sent the Valentine, so I smiled and thanked him for his kind compliments—and then I thanked him for the surprise last week. He looked startled.

"Surprise?"

"The Valentine," I said. "I have guessed right, haven't I? Come, admit it."

A most odd expression came over his face.

"You had a Valentine?" he asked, and I nodded. I got Molly to show it to him, and he looked at it, and ran his fingers over the painted roses. Then he shook his head.

"I'm sorry to disappoint you, Sophy, but it wasn't I who sent it."

"But who can it be?" I burst out.

"Forgive me for asking but—it wasn't young Beaumont from Pengwern?" asked Doctor Hawk, looking worried.

I shook my head, and told him about Charles' visit, when I met Charles by the gate, and told him that he must never come here again. Doctor Hawk looked more and more amazed, but relieved. I think he still suspects that I might be secretly breaking my heart over Charles.

When I had finished, he sat still for a moment, then he said quietly: "You're a surprising young lady, Sophy. I begin to wonder why I was ever worried about you."

Then he bowed over my hand and left. I am sure it must have been him who sent the Valentine, even though he swears not. Who else could it be? I can only think of Mr Prynne-Edwards, and I can hardly imagine him sending a Valentine to somebody in my position, he is so respectable and his family is very strict on social propriety. Still, time will tell.

I spent the rest of the morning after Doctor Hawk had gone, playing the piano and singing. I do not keep up my practising as I should, especially during the winter, because the drawing room is so cold, but it is lovely to have a chance to play, and I enjoyed myself this morning.

After luncheon I went out for my walk. It is still bleak and dreary in the garden, but the birds are chattering louder every day. When Mr Rochester is a little bigger, I will be able to take him on my walks with me, but he is too little. He has settled down quite well, although he woke us up last night by howling in a most pitiful fashion. Molly says he will soon get used to his new home. She came into my room last night with a candle, to tell me not to worry about him, because she had just been down and he was quite all right.

This morning, he seemed better, he even looked pleased to see me when I went into the kitchen, and wagged his tail.

February 23rd

We had another pleasant evening in the drawing room last night, with the fire burning cheerfully. Father and I were both in high spirits, and we presented an impromptu concert for Molly, who came in all of a fluster to sit on the sofa and provide our admiring audience. Robert came too, and sat very stiffly on one of the tapestry chairs.

Father did a very dramatic rendering of Hamlet's famous speech "To be or not to be." He has a magnificent voice, when he can be persuaded to use it—the Antiquarian Society will have a treat when he gives his lecture—and finished up by stabbing himself with an imaginary dagger and dying with convulsive groans.

Then I sang one of the popular romantic songs, with terrific bravura, and Molly and Robert applauded loudly when I had finished. Then Father was persuaded to enact a stern Father, with his new hat on, and an imaginary moustache, and I was the erring daughter, and Molly was brought in to be the housekeeper, and Robert was the village boy who found me drowned in the millpond.

We proceeded very well, except that Molly was too breathless with outrage at being expected to take part in a play, and all she said, when she was supposed to say "Sir Jasper, fling not yon poor erring child into the snow," was: "Well, I don't know—I can't do that," and Robert was just like a log of wood, and when he was supposed to drag me out of the millpond, he swore instead, and then went so red with embarrassment that I had to drag myself out, (it was off the sofa, really).

We all had wine and biscuits afterwards, and Father was in such good spirits that he said we ought to form a company of travelling players, and Molly was very indignant and said: "I've never had any doings with play actors and the likes, Sir John, and never will. How you can think of such things, I don't know, and you a gentleman!"

I am going to continue my history of the house. I am becoming quite an expert on putting facts together. I think my brain must work quite well, even though a woman is not supposed to have one.

February 24th

Father's new coats have come from the tailor's. They are very grand. He had forgotten all about them, and was very surprised when the boy arrived this morning. His lecture is in about two weeks' time, and I am only sorry that I will not be able to go with him, but of course, that could not be possible in my condition. I think it is silly, as I am not in the least likely to faint, but everybody would be so scandalised if I were to appear at a meeting of the Antiquarian Society (which only gentlemen attend anyway) looking rather obviously as though I am having a baby.

Of course, I am getting heavier as the baby grows, and more placid, and I am content to sit here in the old familiar room (Mr Rochester is becoming a very satisfactory companion) and just read and dream—and write in my diary.

I feel like an old grandmother, living on her memories, although mine are not very pleasant ones. When I went away with Charles it was quite dreadful really, most uncomfortable, and then Charles got drunk, and afterwards cried—I don't like to see men crying. I was glad that Father had the sense to realize I was hoping he would come after us and bring me back.

February 25th

It is raining today, the soft misty rain that soaks through everything without one noticing it. The clouds are low on the hills, and we can only just see the poplars, their tops out of sight, reaching up into the mist.

I have been reading all about the Kyffin family who built the house. It is quite exciting—Thomas Kyffin was a sailor with Drake, so I gather, and after the Armada, and Drake's exploits at sea, Kyffin was created Sir Thomas and he came back home wealthy, with his pockets lined with Spanish doubloons, and he built a fine new house for himself and his wife. This part is quite thrilling. Sir Thomas married a Spanish lady. Her name was Doña Inez, and she was from a wealthy family who lived in the Indies (that is, South America). Some of the English seamen raided one of the cities there, and they brought away a lot of treasure, but Sir Thomas brought away Doña Inez, and married her.

It is like a work of fiction—in fact, I have my suspicions that the worthy Mr Duggan who wrote this account, might have been reading too many romances.

February 26th

The mist has closed down on us today and is creeping like a ghost, round the house, blotting out everything. I have not been out this morning, but have been sitting here by the fire, after doing my chores, resting and thinking.

I wonder whether the baby will look like me. If it is a girl, I am calling it Elvira Elizabeth Roy, the Elizabeth after my mother. If it is a boy, I shall call it John Edward Roy—the John is for Father, and the Edward is after Miss Brontë's hero, Mr Edward Rochester.

Speaking of Mr Rochester, my great guard dog has settled down beautifully. He is quite happy now, lord of the kitchen—Molly and Mair spoil him beyond belief, and he lives off the fat of the land. He has his own bed, with an old blanket on it, and he has nearly accepted the idea of the tray of earth, although we have had some upsetting incidents. He is an intelligent little animal, with very bright, alert brown eyes. His coat is dark yellow, like crumpled pansies, but it will become golden brown as he grows. Father says retrievers are very loyal and faithful dogs.

Father was rather amazed when I told him that Mr Prynne-Edwards had been, and brought me a puppy.

"Lies the wind in that quarter, hey?" he said, and lifted his eyebrows.

I don't know what he meant, but I am beginning to suspect that Father reads romantic novels from the circulating library, or at least, that he has a romantic nature. It is all very strange and curious.

I think I will write a note to Mr Prynne-Edwards to tell him that Mr Rochester has settled down. He will be glad to hear that.

They live in a house just out of town, quite a pleasant little mansion, Georgian, much later than this crumbling old pile. I have never been inside it, but the road to town passes their garden, and you can see the roof rising above the trees. It seems a very elegant and cheerful house, and Mr Prynne-Edwards was telling me at the dinner party how from the top floor windows, the view looks out at the back over their garden, with flowerbeds, and then across the fields and meadows, to these hills.

"We can see your house quite clearly, Miss Roy," he said, smiling at me. "It's visible for miles in the valley, you know. When Clarissa and I were children, we used to sit at the window and imagine it a castle of brigands, up in the hills."

I think he must be quite interested in architecture. He told me all about their house being Georgian and described its features.

"It's smaller than your house, of course," he went on, "and not so impressive, I suppose, but Georgian architecture has an elegance and grace of its own. I think you would like it."

Miss Prynne-Edwards looked across, at this, and interrupted our conversation.

"The house is too small altogether," she said, with a petulant line coming between her great blue eyes with their long golden lashes. "I'm trying to persuade Papa to build a new house in the proper style—he has plenty of money, and it would be much the best thing. We are absolutely cramped to death, my dear—" she turned to me at this "—no ballroom, can you imagine? And only five bedrooms, really, Papa has no idea."

"Clarissa wants to create a new Balmoral," said Mr Prynne-Edwards, with an ironic note in his voice.

She fluttered her eyelashes at him and turned back to Father, saying: "Oh, Dick, you are such a tease!" But she was not pleased at his remark, I don't think. Life must be rather difficult for them in their little Georgian mansion.

February 28th

Yesterday was gloomy—another gloomy Sunday—but this morning I woke to a golden day, the light bright and promising, the sun making everything sparkle. My heart felt an immediate lift of spirits and I leaped out of bed—or at least, climbed out rather earlier than usual—to look out across the yard. Robert was already up, I could see him crossing the yard with a pail, and hear Molly singing in the kitchen.

It looked as though this would be a perfect spring day, and Father went out early to the Dyke, the wind lifting his mane of thick hair so that he looked like a lion, and whipping his coat round him in dark folds as he headed for the stile that leads to the path across the field at the back of the copse.

But something has happened that has darkened the day for me. I was out in the yard later this morning, after walking. I had been to see if the daffodils are ready to bloom, but they are not. They are tightly closed, not a sign of the golden crack that will herald the yellow flowers.

I wondered if the daffodils might bloom if we were to bring some of them indoors, and on my way back I went to the yard to look for Robert to ask him, and while we were there standing in a patch of sun near the trough, which is quite green with old age—(it is made out of slabs of stone, grey like the house), there was the sound of a horse's hooves on the path outside the yard, and to my amazement, who should appear in the arch mounted on a beautiful chestnut, but Miss Prynne-Edwards, looking very grand with her yellow curls pulled back under a riding hat with a veil. She was wearing a habit in blue, and looked a picture. I exclaimed with surprise, and went forward to greet her, looking round for her groom and calling Robert to see to her horse.

She dismounted with Robert's help, though swishing her skirt disdainfully away from his corduroy leggings that have a smell of the land about them.

"I have no groom. I came alone," she said, in response to my enquiry. She looked at me—I was wearing my bright plaid dress, with my hair neatly pulled back, and my cloak over my dress. Her lip curled. I saw it distinctly.

"I came to see you," she said, and rather mystified, I asked her to come in. We went into the library, where there was a bright fire, and I asked her to sit down, but she declined, and stood, looking lovely in her trailing habit, snapping her whip against one gloved hand, and looking into the fire.

I sat wondering why she had come. I rang the bell for Molly, and asked her to bring some refreshments. Her eyes went round at the sight of my visitor, and I could imagine the buzz in the kitchen when she went back to fetch the tray with biscuits and tea.

"Will you have some tea?" I asked Miss Prynne-Edwards, as she still showed no inclination to speak. "You must have ridden quite a long way."

Still she was silent, and I went on with a smile: "I am glad to see you. I must apologize about the dinner party, I'm afraid I was rather naughty to tease you about the ghost."

She looked at me, then, and I saw, to my surprise, dislike plain in her blue eyes. But she looked puzzled, too, as though she did not know what to say.

"I was at Pengwern the other day," she said, at last. "I went to call on Christina Beaumont." She paused, then added: "She has been very ill, I suppose you know that?"

"No," I answered, concerned. "No, I had not heard. We are rather sheltered up here, as you can see, we do not hear all the news. I am sorry to hear she has been ill. I trust she is recovered now?"

"No," snapped Miss Prynne-Edwards, still with dislike in her face. "And as far as I can see, she never will. Her husband spends all his time like a moon-sick calf, comparing her to you. Of course, I know all about the—incident last September—" her gaze flicked insolently to my stomach, and, without knowing why, I lifted my hand protectively. She went on: "No, I don't want to stay for your refreshments. I only came to say this.

You've got Charles Beaumont running round in circles, but you're not going to do the same to Dick. I won't let you."

I was so startled, I sat stunned. "To—to Dick?" I faltered at last.

"My brother," she said, and her voice was like dry leaves rasping together. "I hear he brought you a puppy—I saw the innocent note you sent the other day, oh, Miss-Butter-won't-melt-in-my-mouth-Roy—Mr Rochester has settled down very well, has he? 'You must come and see him chasing the snowdrops in the orchard—not to mention imaginary rabbits—' " She hissed a sentence out of my letter to Mr Prynne-Edwards at me, and I felt sick suddenly, and anger stirred in me to see her standing there, filling the peaceful old room with her sharp lemon verbena scent, and tearing the quiet fabric of my day to shreds with her jealous nails.

I stood up and faced her, drawing my shawl round me, and looking squarely into her eyes.

"I don't know how you came to read a private letter written to your brother," I said bluntly. "That does not matter—it is between him and you. But I resent your implications that I am attempting to make Mr Prynne-Edwards run round in circles, as you put it. Nothing could be further from the truth. I respect and like your brother, but that is all."

"I suppose you 'respected and liked' Charles Beaumont, too?" she shrilled, with an ugly inflection in her voice. Molly came in at that moment with a tray, but hearing the sound of our voices, she stopped still, her eyes going wide, and went out again. I don't think Miss Prynne-Edwards even noticed her.

I was growing just as angry now as Miss Prynne-Edwards.

"My relationship with Mr Beaumont is none of your business," I said. "And as for his wife, I am very sorry to hear she has been distressed by his conduct, but if she had any sense at all, she would realize that that would be all she could expect from such a man." I was shaking with anger. "You suggest that I deliberately lured him away from her—that's rubbish. It isn't my fault that he's a philanderer."

"And I suppose it isn't your fault that Dick's a philanderer either?" she flamed, and the dislike in her face had turned to real hate. "Well, I just came to warn you—."

"You can dispense with warnings, thank you, Miss Prynne-

Edwards. I am perfectly capable of conducting my own affairs," I said.

"Affairs?" she laughed coarsely. "Yes—conducting affairs is the right expression. You must have been brought up like a gypsy. What men can see in such vulgar conduct, I really can't imagine."

"Perhaps," I said silkily "they prefer it to your own lady-like behaviour."

For a moment, I thought she would hit me. Then she drew her whip back to her side, and hissed at me: "Just leave Dick alone. Mama's on my side—and Papa will be when he hears. You shan't have Dick."

"I really don't know what you are talking about," I said, clenching my hands in my dress to stop them shaking. "But if that is all you have come to say, I'd be glad if you would take your leave. Good morning."

She glared at me for a moment longer, then swept from the room, and I heard her calling for her horse as she went out. Molly came in, and found me sitting in the leather chair, and she positively clucked with concern.

"In your condition—she needs taking a whip to, does that fine lady."

Robert came in and told us that Miss Prynne-Edwards had ridden off looking like a thunder-cloud, and whipping her horse, poor beast.

I don't know what to think. I feel quite sickened. It is as though she had come in and thrown filth across something beautiful.

March 1st

St David's Day. I woke to see the reflections of sunlight again and the sky a deep clear blue. I looked out of my window before I went down, at the sunlight on the yard, and swathes of light finding their way between the stables and outbuildings. The birds were shrilling their usual morning chorus. They are merry, cheerful little things. I looked out, resting my elbows on the window sill, and let the peace of the day seep into me, the colours splashed with new vividness—spring is really on its way at last.

Inside the house, you can tell that spring is here. The fingers of sunlight are prising their way in everywhere, with motes of dust dancing like gold. There are reflections of light on all sorts of unexpected things, the japanned chair in Father's study, and the glasses in the dining room showered rainbows every time I moved. I feel my blood beginning to stir with the sap of spring. I told Molly this morning that we would start spring-cleaning, and getting the nursery ready. The baby is moving too, more and more energetically, everywhere there is new life.

We spent the morning planning and cleaning; I long to see the house shining like a new pin. Father went out to the Dyke early, and the girls have been chattering like a flock of starlings. I listened to their chattering with a light heart. It is soothing and comforting after the nasty scene of yesterday. I have been trying not to think about it, but it will keep creeping into my mind.

I have thought about what Miss Prynne-Edwards said about Charles' wife. It is very sad, but can I be held responsible for her husband's behaviour? It was not I who made him a philanderer, and I did not attempt to lure him away from his wife. Obviously, though, that is how the rest of society sees it.

I suppose it would have been different if I had been the one to suffer—if I had really loved Charles (heaven forbid). But why is it wrong because I don't feel like that now I know what he is like?

I think I must join Father in taking up a stand against the rest of society. A fig for society! Society be damned! I dislike and despise Clarissa Prynne-Edwards. But I feel—no, I will put the whole thing quite out of my mind. I will not think of Mr Prynne-Edwards. He will never come here again, and I will never see him and I do not care.

Oh, Sophy, you are a liar! I must admit it, I must be honest with myself. I do care. How or why, I don't know. But the thought of Mr Prynne-Edwards makes me happy and sad at the same time. I can't bear that he should think unworthy things of me or see me through his sister's eyes.

Mr Rochester is sitting at my feet, his head resting comfortably on a cleanly picked bone. I sighed and he opened one liquid brown eye and stared at me, then shut it again. There is some comfort in the touch of his soft fur against my ankles.

Later

Fortunately for my peace of mind, there was a distraction at that point. A messenger came from town with Father's order of new books, and I am going to have a treat after tea, I shall commence reading *Wuthering Heights* by Ellis Bell.

March 2nd

I lay awake last night listening to rain pattering on the yard outside, and it must have continued all night for it was still pouring this morning. The day is grey—not very cold, but dismal. The rain has washed the shoots of new flowers to a soft bright green, but the daffodils are still not out, and most of the crocuses are still curled inside the bud.

I have not minded the weather because since last evening I have been reading the novel that came yesterday. It is really magnificent—like poetry, and with such power and force. Wuthering Heights reminds me a little of this house, except that I expect it was more wild. I don't know anybody that compares to Heathcliff. I have not decided yet whether I approve of him or not.

I have been reading all morning since I finished my household chores. Father did not go out on the Dyke, he is in his study. The day of his lecture is tomorrow week. I wondered what might happen as a result of Miss Prynne-Edwards' visit, but it is no use worrying.

How difficult people are. I suppose I must be difficult too, in my own way, but when I think of Charles and Clarissa Prynne-Edwards, their behaviour seems so strange that I can't comprehend it. They must both be unhappy people.

Father is expecting a visitor, I think, Mr Turner, who looks after the estate. They are going to go over the monthly accounts. I never hear much about business, although I am sure it might be quite interesting, but I do look after the household accounts, of course. I keep them up to date all the time, and they are hardly any trouble at all. Father never queries them. He is not interested in money. Fortunately, I have reasonably modest tastes, and so I am able to be economical.

There's a noise in the hall. I must go and see who it is.

It was Mr Turner, of course. He bowed to me, running an inquisitive eye over my gown and shawl, and my hair, which I have done this morning in quite a matronly fashion under a lace cap.

"Ah, Miss Sophy—blooming as ever," he said with a leer—there is no other word for it. Mr Turner is a clever man, and I'm sure must be honest, but he has a regrettably coarse nature where ladies are concerned. I think he tries very hard to be a ladies' man, but it comes out sounding very coarse and unpleasant. However, as I am sure he means well, and is probably lonely for feminine company, I try to be polite to him.

"Good morning, Mr Turner. Father is expecting you," I said,

holding out my hand and smiling.

I took him to the study and called Molly to serve them with port and biscuits, and they are safely closeted there for a few hours, I should think, the rest of the afternoon. I can curl up in my chair and continue my reading in peace.

March 3rd

After a rainy day yesterday which finished with the rain stopping, but everywhere dripping, and all the leafless twigs hung with a bright bauble of water that glittered in the twilight yesterday evening, I awoke this morning to more sun. But we have had frost too, and the lawn is covered with a white layer of hoar frost, the terrace and garden are sparkling, while the park looks a fairyland, hung with frost, mist and sun.

Mr Rochester was lazy this morning, he didn't want to accompany me on my walk. But I put on my bonnet and my old cloak (it is too cold up here on the ridge for shawls), and went out, enjoying the sun and the view. The valley looks beautiful, and in the frosty air one can see for miles, the little toy cottages looking like dolls' houses, their roofs glittering with frost.

Our spring cleaning is going well. I wrapped myself in a voluminous apron of Molly's and went to help the girls. This morning, they have been doing the big painted bedroom—my mother's old room, and the dust flew as they swept and scrubbed. The furniture in that room is black oak, very old, which I helped to polish.

Father says he has no patience with a house full of chattering women, and spring cleaning drives him mad. He went off to the Dyke. I could see him striding across the yard as I was in the kitchen putting on Molly's apron.

I forgot to say that I have been reading some more of *Wuthering Heights*. I am both fascinated and frightened by it. The power in it is so strong and wild, and the writing so beautiful, that it has the effect of a storm, buffeting me until I feel driven before it. I asked Father about it last night. He said the reviews were very bad and the book is considered dangerous. He was quite interested when I told him my own impressions, and nodded sagely when I said I didn't feel it was dangerous, but it is like a wild bird—not the linnet that Doctor Hawk compared me to, but a hawk, or great creature of the moors and fells—struggling to rise from the earth to heaven.

The part where Cathy dies and Heathcliff is grieving for her in the orchard, is so magnificent that it made me cry. I keep feeling as though the keys of life and existence have been put into my hands as I read, and then, when I look away, they have been snatched out of my grasp. I have never felt like this with any other book, not even Sir Walter Scott or Mr Thackeray (I have read *Vanity Fair*, but I didn't like it very much). I have a dreadful feeling that *Wuthering Heights* will not have a happy ending, but I must read on.

I have been neglecting my own writing (if I can call it that) while I read and walk in the garden and help the girls with the cleaning. It says in one of the accounts that the architect who built this house was a very famous man called Inigo Jones. I have discovered, however, that it could not possibly have been built by Inigo Jones, because he was later than Elizabethan. The architect must remain anonymous. Father says that what people used to do in those days was to circulate the plans for a particular house, and all the rich men copied them, with their own additions.

But God bless Sir Thomas Kyffin for deciding to build here! Perhaps, as he had been a sailor with Drake (a "gentleman adventurer," I should think) he was inclined to be restless and so this position, up on the ridge, suited him. He could see for miles and feel free up here.

I wonder how his Spanish wife liked it after her home in the Indies. She must have loved him a great deal to come to what would have seemed to the other side of the world, to live in a strange land and amongst people whom she had been taught to regard as enemies. I can imagine her in her farthingale and ruff, coming down the stairs, speaking to her servants in a soft Spanish voice, in broken English, and then coming out to sit in the garden with her embroidery.

What a romantic story! I wonder if I would ever be able to love a man as much as that?

I think that really, men are just the same as women. I mean, I know they are bigger and stronger, and have more courage in battle, and things like that, but they seem to me to make mistakes and be afraid of things just as women are. Even Father, of whom I am very fond, was not very brave about my mother dying. I can understand that he was upset, but it does seem a little extravagant to shut yourself up for the rest of your life. After all, life is for us to live.

And then Charles, I am sure, is more of a fool and a coward than practically any woman I can think of (except, possibly Miss Jones). When I compare Charles with his birth and breeding and his money, with somebody like, say, Miss Angharad from the village who has to struggle to keep body and soul together (as Molly would put it) Charles does not come off very well.

I mean, to marry somebody you don't love, and then to tell somebody else that you are passionately in love with her, and persuade her to run away with you is not a very sensible thing to do.

We eventually got to Chester, where Charles was planning to take the railway to London or somewhere a long way off, but as his main purpose in our running away had been for him to seduce me, he delayed our catching the train until the next day, and we were received at the hotel by the station as Mr and Mrs Charles Beaumont.

I would have preferred the excitement of a journey on the railway, because the seduction part didn't interest me very much, but by the next morning, of course, Father had come galloping into the yard with Robert, and stamped up the stairs, sweeping the servants out of the way, to find me and take me home.

I can't say how glad I was to hear his voice bellowing: "Where is she? Where's my daughter?" because by then, Charles had fallen in a fit of self-remorse, and had cried and asked whether I could ever forgive him, and I was so hurt at his faithless behaviour that I had decided to go home anyway.

March 4th

I went out this morning, blustered about by the wind, to find lambs' tails fluttering like yellow rain in the copse, and daisies with little red-tipped petals beginning to open on the lawn.

The weather has been most unpredictable today. We have had rain, sweeping across and battering on the windows, and then sun, all the clouds clearing and the sky suddenly blue. This afternoon I went out—drawn by the sun—and no sooner had I got outside than the rain came down and the sky was dark.

I watched the long drops lashing the windows in the White Room, blurring everything, and then quite suddenly it was all over and while the sun was brilliant over towards the west with a sort of golden haze in the sky, making the poplars look like something out of a dream, misty and outlined in gold; the sky was quite dark on the other side of the valley, with the gulls, who have been flying inland, like pieces of white paper against it. And the park all vivid green, like my dinner dress, soft and velvety, the light so clear.

I called Molly out just in time to see a rainbow, or half of it, in a great curve dipping down over the valley. It ended just where the Twelve Disciples stand at the bottom of the park, near the well. They are called that although there are thirteen—plane trees—and they surround the Bath House, where the people who used to live here used to bathe. We don't use it now, of course, because we have water in the house, and it is rather a ruin, but very picturesque. I wonder if we dug under the old bath, would we find the crock of gold at the end of the rainbow?

I have read some more of *Wuthering Heights*, and it makes me feel both exhilarated and miserable by turns. I have also been bustling about quite a lot, helping the girls, and Molly has threatened to send for Doctor Hawk. She says I should rest, but I'm as jumpy as a rabbit today. Father got soaking wet on the Dyke, and I am afraid he may catch a chill and not be able to attend his lecture on Wednesday—that would be a terrible calamity, and I scolded him and made him wrap up and sit by the fire and drink a hot toddy.

Mair says there was an accident at the Works yesterday—the Works which Mr Prynne-Edwards is connected with, I mean. Her cousin Benny is employed there. It sounds dreadful—something blew up, but only one man was hurt, and not seriously.

I have also read a little more of my history of the house—I have reached the war between King Charles and Parliament, when the last Kyffin heir was killed at Rowton Heath, before the King retreated to Denbigh. I have found out why people say the house was designed by Inigo Jones. It is because somebody in the reign of James I did some alterations, so the architecture is really a mixture of Elizabethan and what is called Jacobean. I told Father, and he was very interested. I told Molly and she told me that too much reading in books would give me brain fever.

March 5th

We had a surprise this morning. It looked a gloomy day when I got up, but while I was having breakfast I looked out of the window, and to my amazement, saw, of all things—snow! From a few drifting feathers, the world became full of whirling flakes, as big as sovereigns, that covered up the garden like a blanket, and lodged in the bare twigs of the trees. I wonder if we will be snowed up. We have been very lucky so far this year, with only a couple of snowfalls, very light, but the house is surrounded now by a soft white blanket a few inches thick, and Mair and Shan came scrambling through the snow this morning, with their faces shining with exertion and white flakes powdering their hair and shawls.

We have been continuing the spring cleaning intermittently, and the house is beginning to look sparkling. The nursery for the baby is waiting to be redone in pleasant colours (it is now covered by some hideous wallpaper) and decorated with Noah's Ark figures. I can imagine them parading in twos round the walls—lions and tigers, bears and elephants, and Noah and his family.

The old cot where I used to sleep when I was a baby is so awful I am going to get Robert to chop it up for firewood. My mother was so ill that she never had time to prepare a pretty cradle for me, or a proper nursery. Molly says a big drawer from the chest of drawers would do but I am determined that little Elvira shall have a cradle with ribbons and bows—or if it is a boy, a nice one trimmed with blue. I think I will engage Mair—if she will agree—to be nursemaid. Mair is an honest, hard-working little thing, faithful and loyal and cheerful, and she would be so proud to have a position, instead of being a sort of maid-of-all-work as she is now.

I have been rather worried today about Father. He has a cough that he caught yesterday on the Dyke, and his chest is sore this morning. I tried to get him to stay in bed today with a fire in his room, but he insisted on getting up, and is in the study, sorting his notes ready for the great lecture on Wednesday evening. It is entitled "Offa's Dyke—glimpses of a historic past," and is all about the things he has dug up on the Dyke.

Mr Rochester has been out with me today, we didn't go out for long, but he played with great delight with the snowflakes, chasing them and barking enthusiastically. He is becoming quite beautifully trained in the house now—or almost! I think he must be a dog with a particularly bright intellect. I had never realized before how much companionship an animal can give.

I have been wondering, in odd moments, what Miss Prynne-Edwards did after she went away the other day. There has been no message or anything, no news from town at all, no gossip about the family from Mair and Shan. Perhaps she came up here on the spur of the moment and was sorry afterwards. I hope so.

March 6th

So much for my hopes of being snowed-up. It had all gone by yesterday evening. But we have had rather a day today, Father's chest is a little worse, although he swears there is nothing to worry about. His chill has made him morbid. He expressed a sudden desire this morning to go and see my mother's grave. It is a lovely day, with signs of spring everywhere, and the sun coming and going. I pointed out, though, that it was Sunday, and that the people would be going to Church, and also that it would be better to leave it until his chill was better.

"Nonsense, Sophy," he growled. "I've left her alone all these years, I won't leave her a minute longer."

And he gave orders for Robert to get the carriage ready. Well, I insisted on going with him, and at last he in his new coat and high hat, me in my new bonnet and cloak and Robert very grand in his new boots, we set out after luncheon at a steady pace suitable for Sunday.

Fortunately, the people were all at the afternoon service. Robert stayed with the carriage at the church gates, and I got out to go with Father down the path and round to the grave-yard at the back. I was very curious. I had never seen my mother's grave before. I took Father's arm, and we walked down the path and round the western end of the church, while inside, the people sang, we could hear their voices and the sound of the organ.

Father stopped before a great tomb almost like a little house. My mother lies in a marble confine, with a weeping lady at her side, and an angel with a sword at her head. It is no wonder that Father has never been—I am sure all this magnificence must have been arranged by someone else, not him at all. The stone says: "Here lies Elizabeth, beloved wife of Sir John Roy, Bart, died October 2nd 1837, aged 22 years."

Father stood quite still, looking at the grave, then he nodded once or twice and turned away. I went to take his arm, and we walked back to the carriage without saying anything. He said nothing on the way home either, and when Robert turned the carriage into the yard, he got out and went into the house and shut himself in the study. Molly took him some mulled wine at my instructions, and she reported that he was sitting in the big chair by the fire, looking quite cheerful and peaceful.

"Had his eyes shut, he did," she said, when she came out. "You mark my words, miss, it's a sign. He'll be the next to go, it must have been Miss Elizabeth's spirit calling to him from the grave, made him want to go to the churchyard. He'll not last long."

She was so bothered that she fussed round Father and actually made herself late for chapel. I went into the study afterwards to see if Father wanted anything.

"Has she gone?" he demanded, without looking up. "Thank heaven. She'll worry me into my grave."

"She thinks you were prompted to visit the churchyard by a call from Beyond," I explained. "She's afraid you'll be leaving us for the next world quite soon."

He snorted. "Never felt fitter. Come and sit with me for a little while, will you, Sophy?"

So we sat in the firelight and he spoke to me about my mother, just a few sentences at random, but he has never done it before. He patted my hand as I got up to light the lamps and smiled at me, and I felt quite suddenly as though I wanted to cry, but for happiness not sadness. I can't explain it, but I felt very close to Father, and to my mother as well, though she is dead. I felt far more understanding about how Father has suffered all these years. He loved her so much. I had never thought before, but loving brings pain with it too. I wonder if I will ever be brave enough to really love anybody.

March 7th

Father woke up this morning and his voice is only a croak. Molly has dosed him with cough mixture, honey, and whisky and hot water, but he still can't speak. He is very irritable and declares he feels perfectly well otherwise, so he got up and came down to the study. I am rather bothered because his lecture is the day after tomorrow, and if he can't speak, he won't be able to go. I am going to send Robert with a note to Mr Prynne-Edwards—very private, to be delivered only to him— I don't want Miss Prynne-Edwards interfering again. I can hardly believe that he showed her my letter about Mr Rochester, and unworthy as the thought may be, I am forced to conclude that she snoops amongst his papers.

I have just been down with Molly to the well. The day is moist but lovely and balmy. It was damp and muddy in the park, and I stayed on the path while Molly went to the well. It is where we get our water for drinking. We have water in the house, but it is not used for drinking, only for washing.

The well is built in the side of a little hill. There is a spring, which never dries up, and a basin below into which it flows, then it runs down the slope of the park like a stream. The water is pure and fresh and always very cold, even on the hottest day in summer. It usually gets muddy around the well, and we have stepping stones to get to it.

I remember that once, I got into disgrace for pushing Miss Jones so that she fell into the mud and dirtied her new sprigged muslin gown. I was shut up in my room without fire or candle all evening—Father was away in town for some reason—but when he came back and Molly told him what Miss Jones had done, he lost his temper and roared and told her to let me out at once, and said if she did it again, she would have to go. Then she said she had got to be able to discipline me.

"The child is like a gypsy," she said, standing facing Father with two spots of red on her cheeks. "She is spoiled and selfish." Then two tears trickled down her long sheep's face and her lip trembled. "My new gown—wore it for the first time this afternoon, and—all her fault—utterly ruined—"

Molly remembers the scene quite well. Father sent for me from my room, and frowned sternly at me, and demanded whether I had indeed spoiled Miss Jones' gown.

"It was a game, Father," I said, standing with my hands behind my back. "We were seeing who could keep their footing on the stones—and Miss Jones couldn't. She fell into the mud."

"You pushed me, Sophy. You did indeed," sobbed Miss Jones, into her handkerchief.

Molly says she saw a twinkle come into Father's eye, but when he spoke, his voice was still stern.

"You shall be recompensed, Miss Jones. I will give you a cheque to buy a new gown. And as for you, Sophy, you will apologize immediately."

"Yes Father," I said obediently, and turned to Miss Jones. "I wish to apologize—" I began, but at the sight of Miss Jones with her red watery eyes, her face raddled with tears, her hair coming loose in wisps from her cap, I burst into tears myself, and threw both arms round her.

"Oh, dear, dear Miss Jones, I'm so dreadfully sorry. I am. I am. You can have my new white muslin dress, or you could if it would fit you, and when I am to have a new dress next time, you must have one instead, she can, can't she Father? And I'll wear my old ones for ever and ever."

Miss Jones hugged me and I hugged her, and we both sobbed together.

"Spoiled—but not entirely selfish," said Father. "No more punishment for her I beg Miss Jones, I don't want her conscience to become unduly developed. We are not Methodists yet, thank God."

"And what he meant by that I don't know," Molly finished, with a sniff, when she was telling me that story.

Robert has just been in to take my message for Mr Prynne-Edwards. I told him to deliver it personally.

March 8th

What a day today has been. I will remember it always. The eighth of March. But I don't know whether it is a sad day or a happy one.

It started off as usual more or less. Father's voice is still a croak, and he has got into the habit of banging with his stick on the floor to make us hear if he wants anything. It is like having a gouty old gentleman in the house.

I got up a little later than usual. I have not been sleeping very well for the last few days, and also I have been feeling a little tired, on account of the baby, I expect. But it has been quite a long winter, though a moderate one, and I will be glad to see the spring and the summer coming. Molly has succumbed at last to a cold, and I am afraid, what with Father's chest and Molly's head-cold, the house is dismal and I expect it will be my turn next. Shan came in as usual to help us this morning, but Mair has got a chill and had to stay in bed. I will go over and see her, perhaps, tomorrow, if she is no better.

But this morning. I was in the garden, walking rather disconsolately in the orchard, with my cloak wrapped round me against the raw air, when I saw Shan hurrying down the steps, her face very red.

"Oh, Miss," she gasped. "A gentleman come to see you, there is, and I can't find Molly, and Sir John—"

I interrupted the flow of words, for hard on her heels, I saw Mr Prynne-Edwards coming down the path, in a fine black broadcloth coat, his hat in his hand.

"It's all right, Shan," I said. "Go back inside and put out the port and some biscuits in the drawing room will you? There's a fire there today because Doctor Hawk is coming later on."

"Yes Miss," she gasped, and with a glance at Mr Prynne-Edwards, she scuttled back up the steps like a frightened rabbit.

He came towards me, and stood in front of me. His head caught one of the spread branches of an apple tree, and it showered him with drops of water, glittering on his fair hair.

"Mr Prynne-Edwards—I hardly expected that you would call in person," I began. "Won't you come in?"

"Perhaps—In a moment, but first I have something to say to you alone, Miss Roy," he answered, and there was a note in his voice that made me look up quickly.

"I understand that Clarissa came and—and tried to frighten you with threats." His face was stern. He seemed much taller than I remembered, and his eyes were very blue.

"Miss Prynne-Edwards called," I began, not knowing what to say. "But she—I mean—I haven't—"

I felt my face burn crimson as I thought of what she had said about him, and I turned away, for I could not bear to think that he thought the same way of me.

He saw my face and took one of my hands, pulling me round to look at him.

"Miss Roy—Sophy—"

I looked up, and he looked back at me. Then he said quietly: "Whatever they say, whatever they do, nothing will alter the way I feel about you."

I felt as though I was sinking into a mist, drowning in the look in his eyes. "What do you mean?" I said faintly.

"That I love you," he said, still holding my hand. Then, as I stared at him, he leaned forward and kissed me, very gently, on the lips. It was a soft touch like the brushing of a butterfly's wing, oh, so sweet and so tender and so quickly gone.

I pulled my hand away, feeling myself swept up in a turmoil, and angry suddenly.

"How dare you, Mr Prynne-Edwards? I would have expected it from someone else, but not from you. I thought you—I thought you were different," I finished, feeling as though I wanted to cry.

"I love you truly, Sophy," he said steadily. "I know I am not worthy of you, but—"

"Not worthy of me? How can you—joke like that," I said, realising suddenly what I had done. I indicated myself bitterly.

"I am—as you know well—"

"I know everything, Sophy. But it makes no difference to me. You are you, and I love you." The sky was as blue through the branches of the apple tree, as his eyes, clear and warm, so I felt the tears coming again, and I clutched my cloak round me, trying to stop my hands shaking, and turned my head away so that he should not see I was crying.

He stood for a few moments, looking at me, then, very quietly, he said, "I have to go to Staffordshire on business this afternoon. I may not be back for some days."

But still I did not answer, and he looked at me for a few moments longer, then he said: "Take care of yourself."

I saw him turn, and replace his hat as he went with an easy stride up the steps and round to the yard where his horse waited. He didn't look back, and I stood for a long time where he had left me, with the raindrops dripping from the gnarled branches of the fruit trees onto my head, like tears, as the sounds of his horse's hooves died away along the drive. Then everywhere was still.

PART THREE

March 13th

I went out this morning for the first time for nearly a week. Oh, the beauty of it all! The tide has really turned at last—some of all colour crocuses are out—white, mauve and masses of gold—like jewels, they are so bright. The daffodils are budding and I found one nearly out. And I think that the old cherry tree is beginning to blossom, tiny stars of white are appearing on the lower branches. Leaves are everywhere now, new green, and in the park I can see flecks of gold—celandine and dandelion. There is purple heather out in the rockery, and little blue anemonies.

Molly told me I shouldn't go out yet, but the day is so beautiful, with the sun really out, and in the light everywhere a glitter and a brightness. There is a wind, tossing the washing in the orchard, a friendly wind, such as we have not had all these long months, a rascally wind, flurrying the heads of the flowers, and calling everything to awake, because spring is here.

I put my old warm cloak on and my bonnet, and walked very slowly, not hurrying, out into the garden and stood for a while on the lawn, just drinking everything in, feeling strength coming back to me. Then I went down the steps to the orchard, and stood there, and it was as though I had been dead, and come alive again.

I stood in the place where Mr Prynne-Edwards was when he came last week, but only the little wind was there playing in the boughs of the fruit trees, and the sun very warm.

After he had gone, I don't know how I managed to get back up to the house, for though of course I didn't know it at the time, I was quite ill. The sickness that had already attacked Father and Molly had made an assault on me too, no wonder that I behaved so strangely, for I was feeling dreadful by the time Doctor Hawk came in the afternoon, and I hadn't been able to eat any luncheon at all. Doctor Hawk took a look at me, lying on the *chaise longue* in the drawing room, huddled as close as I could to the fire, and said to Molly, who had come in with him: "Get her to bed."

While they were putting a fire in my room, and warming the bed, he sat with me in the drawing room, and I remember that I felt so dreadful that I began to cry and sobbed out the story of what had happened in the orchard. He held my hand and patted my shoulder, looking terribly concerned.

"Dick Prynne-Edwards? But why should this have upset you, child? He is a fine man, none better."

"I know—that's just it—he is so good and well respected and everything—the whole thing is impossible."

"Impossible? My dear Sophy, why?"

"Oh, you know why," I sobbed passionately. "Nobody like him could ever love somebody in—in my condition. And I'm not going to marry anybody. I want to stay here with Father and Molly and Elvira—"

"Who is Elvira?" questioned the doctor. I think he thought my mind was wandering.

"I'm going to call the baby Elvira, if it is a girl." I was shivering by now, and my teeth were chattering. "Elvira Elizabeth—the Elizabeth is after my mother."

"And if it is a boy? One can't always guarantee satisfaction you know and I would advise you not to set your mind on having a girl," said Doctor Hawk, rubbing my hands.

"I—haven't. I shan't mind a boy," I got out, through my chattering teeth. "I'll call it John Edward."

Molly came in at that moment to say that my room was all ready, and they helped me to my feet and up the stairs. My legs felt like jelly, and I was glad of Doctor Hawk's strong arm round my waist.

"John—after your Father," he said, as we were going. "Why Edward?"

"After Mr Rochester—Miss Brontë's hero in *Jane Eyre*," I managed to reply, and I saw his mouth twitch. But my head was whirling, and it felt as though iron bands were tightening round it. I also felt deathly sick. Molly says I was green by the time I got to bed.

"Like an old cheese," she added. What a horrible thought!

I can't remember very much more of that awful afternoon. They put me to bed and I was wrapped up in warmth and comfort. Doctor Hawk seemed very concerned, and told Molly to keep me quiet, and as he was going out he stopped by the door and said, to Molly, very quietly: "Look after her. She's only a child herself."

Then I think I fell asleep, and woke at intervals, to become aware of the red glow from the fire, and Molly sitting near me, knitting the fleecy white shawl she is making for the baby. It was strange to be in bed in the middle of the day, hearing sounds from the yard outside and Robert's boots on the cobbles. Later that day it began to rain, and the long needles pattered on the window, so Molly drew the curtains and lit the lamp they had brought up. Father appeared a few times. He was not feeling very well himself, and was very worried about me.

Robert came in once or twice with coal for the fire. I was aware of his making efforts not to disturb me, but he made more noise than ever with his loud breathing as he tried to walk on his toes.

I got up the day before yesterday for a few hours, and yesterday I was up most of the day, but I insisted on coming out today because the weather is so beautiful. I do admit though, to feeling a little tired now, and I am going to sit all the rest of the afternoon with my feet up, reading the remaining part of *Wuthering Heights*. I still have not quite finished it. Mr Rochester can keep me company. He had missed me, so Molly said, and went sniffing round the library looking for me.

March 14th

I am glad I didn't miss yesterday, with its sudden upsurge of golden light. Today is cold, so cold that I am wondering whether we are going to have some more snow. There is no sun either, the day is solidly grey and even the garden has lost its colour.

I have begun to gather the threads of the household together again after being ill. Molly's head-cold was only a slight one and she gave herself so many herbal remedies that it has gone now. I have been drinking some of her herbal tea in order to please her.

Father is much better. His voice is nearly back to normal and he is bustling about with a light in his eye that is most unlike him. He is up to something, I am sure, but what it is I don't know, and he is having as much pleasure as a child in keeping the secret from me. Molly knows what it is, and I have intercepted so many meaning glances between them that it is becoming quite monotonous, but I shan't ask. No doubt he will tell me in good time.

He wrote a letter to Mr Prynne-Edwards and the Antiquarian Society, apologizing for being unable to attend and give his lecture. I have not told him yet what passed in the orchard before I was ill. I have not been able to sort it out in my own mind. It seems like a far-away dream now, and I go hot and red when I think of it. What is the matter with me? It must be some weakness of spirit after being ill. I have never felt like this ever before.

Doctor Hawk called this morning to check on my progress. He seemed very pleased with me. He says I am perfectly all right, and so is the baby, for which I was glad. He asked me whether I feel better now about Richard Prynne-Edwards, and I know I blushed scarlet red, like my flannel petticoat.

"There's nothing to feel better about," I said firmly. "I don't suppose he will come here again."

"There's talk in the town—how he means to marry you," said Doctor Hawk, quietly.

I felt a sort of rage begin to burn inside me. "How dare they! I have never agreed to any of it. I didn't encourage him—I hate him for making me the object of gossip—I shall never speak to him ever again—I—I'll send Mr Rochester back—"

I only stopped when I ran out of breath, and lay there panting with fury, while Doctor Hawk's mouth twitched in a half-smile that made me feel more furious than ever.

"I have no recollection of such a display of exquisite anger when Charles Beaumont was the man involved," he said.

"That was different," I flashed, before I had time to think. "He didn't matter."

"Ah!" he nodded, and got up to leave me, looking quite pleased.

"I don't care two pins for Mr Prynne-Edwards," I said. "And you can tell the gossips that."

He laughed then, fondly, like a parent indulging a favourite child.

"There's none so blind," he quoted twinkling at me as he bowed his leave. Then he added: "But don't get too overwrought, Sophy, I beg you. I don't want to be called out to deliver your child before its time."

I am quite bothered at the idea that I am being talked about in town. That is really rather strange, because it has never worried me before. I feel quite odd, most unlike myself.

Mair has recovered and is back with us. She is a little paler than usual, and I have told Molly to give her a drop of wine with her dinner each day for a week or two, to get the colour back in her cheeks. Shan has been carrying on heroically, I find, during the time I was upstairs. She is only a little thing, but she nerved herself for the crisis and more than pulled her weight with Molly ill and Mair away.

I have decided to raise their wages, and give them proper status, Mair as housemaid and Shan as kitchen maid. They will have all the usual things—holidays and half-days—that the best people give their servants. I have been very lax in my treatment of them, of course, we have not had any proper servants for years, and I have not had to deal with them, only Molly and Robert, and they are more like family. Mair and Shan can have the two bedrooms down the corridor from mine, and I know it is a little irregular, but they are preparing the rooms themselves this afternoon. They are both thrilled at the idea of coming "into service" properly, and actually living in the house.

I also mentioned to Mair about making her nursemaid when the baby is born, and her little freckled face shone.

"Oh—miss! D'you mean it, really?"

"Of course I do," I said. "I'm sure you will be a very good nursemaid."

"Well, there's four little 'uns at home," she blurted, going pink. "But miss—I mean—you know, with your dad being Sir John—"

"Loyalty and willingness to please make up for all sorts of things," I said, smiling at her. "I'd far rather have you in charge of the baby than some starched nursemaid from London, Mair. We're friends, aren't we?"

She blushed pink again, and swallowed. "Yes miss," she said, as though I'd conferred a great honour onto her, and she almost skipped out of the room.

I have finished *Wuthering Heights*. What a marvellous, magnificent work! I cried at the end, but out of joy, or something like it. Contrary to my expectations, the ending is happy, so happy, and full of hope that I almost couldn't bear it. I am so glad that Cathy and Hareton will be able to live with the shadow of Heathcliff removed from their lives.

March 15th

It rained last night, I could hear it pattering on the window. I like the sound of rain when I am snugly tucked up in bed with the covers round my ears. Sometimes we have storms, great storms that sweep across the valley. They can be terrible up here in our exposed position, but I don't really mind them. The house has stood for centuries, withstanding everything, and I feel that its walls protect us.

When I got up, the rain had stopped. It is quite a dull day. I am still taking things quietly. I did the accounts this morning at the writing table in the library, as usual, and this afternoon, after a walk in the garden, I am sitting resting.

Father is still busy with his secretive activities. What can they be? I am becoming quite intrigued, but he is enjoying himself so much that I must wait patiently. I suddenly remembered that it will be his birthday at the end of this month. I must plan a really pleasant surprise. Normally we do not make much of them, and except for my ball last birthday we have just a small celebration dinner. Last year, I gave Father a paper weight with fossils in it (it was a lump of quartz from one of the quarries, which I had secretly commissioned Robert to get for me from a friend of his who works there.)

Later

While I was deep in contemplation of what to give Father for his birthday, Robert arrived from town with letters. There were several for Father, which are waiting for him in the hall until he comes back from the Dyke (he is investigating a Roman midden, apparently, at present) and there was a letter for me.

It was from Mr Prynne-Edwards. Straight away, as soon as I

saw it, I recognised the handwriting that was on my Valentine! So now the mystery is solved at last. It was Mr Prynne-Edwards who sent it. I suppose I have really known for some time, although I have not admitted it. I came into the library to open the letter, where I could be quite alone, half-afraid of what he might have written.

It was sent from Wolverhampton where he is at present. I think it is a love-letter, the first one I have ever had. I don't know whether I am pleased or dismayed. I am a fallen woman now—an outcast of polite society, and I feel as though I have been trapped—not by somebody else, as Doctor Hawk said when he compared me to a wild bird in a cage—but by my own nature and what I have done.

I must admit, however, that I admire Mr Prynne-Edwards' steadfast but quiet determination. He is as true and loyal as Sir Galahad, although I fear his ideal is not quite so worthy as the Holy Grail. He has taken great care not to upset me in this letter, and has even refrained from calling me Sophy.

"My dear Miss Roy"—how stilted and formal it sounds. "I trust you are well and happy. I hope I did not cause you undue pain at our last meeting, and I feel I must reassure you that I would never make you suffer or force you to accept something that made you unhappy, if it was in my power to prevent such a thing.

"I am at present in Staffordshire, as you will see from the post mark, but hope to be returning home shortly. I trust your Father is recovered from his indisposition—"

March 16th

Father's secret has been revealed! This morning, two workmen arrived from town with rolls of wallpaper to decorate the nursery suite. Father had planned it all while I was ill, he and Molly had put their heads together to find something that would please me.

The workmen, who are called Gwilym and Glyn, have been backwards and forwards mixing their paste for the paper-hanging, and singing to each other as they work. The house seems to be waking to a new existence, what with their voices upstairs, and Mair and Shan chattering for all the world like two starlings in the kitchen.

Molly looked so gratified at my expression when the workmen came, that I think she will be in a good mood for several weeks on the strength of it. I have asked her to make a special dinner for Father's birthday. We will have all his favourite things, and have the dining-room polished up, and flowers, and make a real occasion of it.

Thinking about a special dinner made me think of our dinner party and Mr Prynne-Edwards' letter, which I had forgotten in the excitement. I thought about it as I walked in the garden after luncheon.

The garden was like something from a fairy-tale, with silvery mist hanging like webs over the grass and trees and cutting off the tops of the poplars. Strange how quiet this weather is—the air was quite deadened when I went away from the house, with only the crack of a twig or the sigh of a leaf brushing against my skirt to break the stillness. But as I came back, I heard voices from the nursery suite penetrating even through the closed windows. Gwilym and Glyn have fine voices—tenor and counter-tenor—and there was a cheerful clatter of their buckets and ladders as I came through the hall.

I have just been interrupted by Molly coming in to make sure the fire is still burning brightly. She looked pleased to see me resting and went out again, but I can hear Father's footsteps coming from the study, they sound quite purposeful. He is calling me!

March 17th

The most thrilling thing has happened! Father has finished his book about King Offa and the Dyke! I suppose it was inevitable that he would finish it one day, but he has been working on it for so long that I had never expected that it would come to an end.

There was chattering all round when everybody heard about it. Molly thinks Father is unique anyway, and Mair and Shan, who can hardly read, were so overcome with awe, you would have thought Father was some sort of god and they were going to bow down and worship him.

"But what are you going to do with it, Father?" I asked, when the first excitement was over.

Father said he didn't know, but while we were having supper, I remembered that he told me once about a friend of his, who was at school with him, who is a publisher in London. Father looked pleased, but doubtful, and I had to set to and persuade him that the best thing to do would be to go to London himself and see this friend.

Well, Father didn't need much persuading really, and this morning, we have been busy getting ready for him to go, dragging his box down from the boxroom and packing, and Molly has been washing and ironing his shirts and Robert has been sent off post-haste to town to get some new pocket handkerchiefs.

He didn't want to leave me alone at first, but Doctor Hawk arrived in the middle of the bustle—I had quite forgotten that he was coming today—and he was delighted to hear about Father finishing the book, and agreed with me that I would be perfectly all right while Father was away.

In all the excitement, the paper-hanging in the nursery suite has taken on secondary importance. I went up after Doctor Hawk had gone, and Father was in his study going over the manuscript, to see how it was progressing. The rooms are beginning to look really charming.

March 18th

In the crisp light of early morning we were all up today getting Father ready to be off to London. Molly almost wept as the carriage rumbled off along the drive, with Robert very stiff and important on the box and Father waving to us out of the window. He nearly lost his new hat by waving it, but fortunately, managed to recover it in time.

The house seems strangely empty without him, although quite often, I never have sight nor sound of Father from when he goes out to the Dyke until late in the evening.

We still have company, however, in the form of our two black-haired, merry-eyed paper-hangers, who gave me a wonderful rendering this morning (in harmony) of the lovely ballad *Myfanwy*. I am sorry to say that poor little Mair has quite fallen in love with Gwilym—sorry because I found out through questioning Molly, who generally knows everything, that he has a wife already and three small children and a fourth on the way. So there is no hope for Mair there.

The girls have settled in from yesterday, and they are delighted to have a room of their own each, even though the rooms are quite small and the furniture is not very grand. But I am wondering whether it would have been better for them to share a room, for Shan, who is only a baby really, disturbed Molly in the night with sobbing and when Molly went to see what the matter was, Shan had her head down under the sheets and swore she had seen a light moving in the room and heard a strange noise, and she sobbed out: "Oh! It's a *bwgan*!" (That is, a sort of ghost.)

Molly was quite unmoved by poor Shan's fears at sleeping in a room she thinks is haunted by a *bwgan*. She has always maintained very stoutly (when I was a little girl and I was afraid of the dark steps down into the cellar) that: "You'll never meet anything worse than yourself!"

But I think something must have been walking in the house last night, some restless spirit, for apart from Shan's "*bwgan*" I had a strange dream. I did not remember it when I woke up, it wasn't until just now, after luncheon, that it suddenly popped back into my head. I dreamed that I was dead and my ghost was haunting the house, and floating about outside the windows and in the copse and the park and gardens, and then some people came and I knew they were going to destroy the house. In the dream I tried to plead with them to spare it, but they could not hear my cries, and they took no notice and I ran frantically about, to and fro, in and out of the rooms, and up the stairs, and all the time I knew that soon something would happen and I would be left to wander in the dark for ever and never have a place to rest for the house would be gone.

And then I saw it gone, the hill was still here, with a winter wind howling and snow coming from the north, and the trees in the copse lashing and whipping and crying out with the wind, and the sound was like voices of devils and lost souls. And the place where the house had stood was all dark and desolate, with the snow beginning to cover the earth and the wind blowing the flakes across the ground like little scurrying animals running away in terror.

I was not afraid in my dream, I stood at the end of the drive, with the poplars on each side, and there was nothing at all but a great misery and desolation, and the sound of the wind and the whisper of the snow.

It was so real that just writing about it has made me feel in the grip of the same misery and desolation now. I look up to see the flames burning brightly in the fireplace, and the light flickering on my crocuses, and Mr Rochester, with his soft fur against my feet. I can hear Molly's voice and the creaking of her stays as she comes through the hall. Later she will bring tea and scones with new bread (she has been baking this morning, to take her mind off Father's departure) and some of my favourite ginger cake.

I hope Father is all right. It seems strange to think that he will be sleeping somewhere away from the house tonight.

March 19th

As Molly is always saying, "It never rains, but it pours." What with Father away, I hoped things might be quiet, but this very morning, when I was doing the accounts in the library, Mair came in full of importance to announce: "A gentleman to see you, miss."

It was Mr Prynne-Edwards. I thought at first he had come to see Father, and told him that Father is in London. He was very interested to hear that the book is finished, but he looked at me very hard and said: "That is unfortunate—your Father being away, I mean. I hoped I might have spoken to him—on a matter of supreme importance to me."

I could feel myself going red. He looked round the library (Mair had withdrawn) and came forward and caught my hand—my left hand, I was holding my pen in the other.

"Say I may speak to your Father, Sophy," he said, very low. "I have thought of you constantly while I was away."

"It's—not possible," I said, but my heart was pounding so fast that the words came out in little spurts, like jets of water, and my voice sounded strange, not at all like my own.

"I know that I love you," he insisted. And, still holding my hand, he went on, in a husky voice: "Until I met you, I had always thought I would have to marry somebody like Clarissa. She has her faults, I know, but she is no better and no worse than most of the eligible young ladies Mama is for ever throwing at my head. But when I saw you—at your ball last year—."

I nodded. Somehow, we were sitting, I on my leather chair, he on the arm of it, looking down into my face.

"I knew you were the one I wanted to marry," he continued. "You, and only you. You are so—so different to the others, so vivid. In that red gown, you looked like an enchantress of old, strayed into this century from the pages of Malory, or the French romances, like the Lady Vivian, from the stories of King Arthur. I read them with Mr Poole when I was a boy, and I have never forgotten them."

"You must not," I interrupted, pulling my hand away and standing up. "Please go. I cannot marry you."

"You mean—because of—Charles Beaumont?" he asked, and in such a tender voice that I felt the tears spring to the back of my eyes and the room blurred. He had risen too, and he turned me gently round to face him. "Sophy—."

And then, as though he could not help it, he drew me into his arms, and held me against him. I could feel his heart beating and the strength of his body, and smell the fine scents of good linen and broadcloth and cologne water.

I was trembling and he held me close and then kissed my mouth, not like in the orchard, but with fire on his lips, that spread down from my mouth right through me and made me feel as though my whole body was crimson with blushes. It was so beautiful and hurtful at once, that I reacted in a way that I am horrified to remember.

I pulled myself free and slapped his face, or tried to, but I forgot that I was still holding the pen, and all that happened was that a great blob of ink splashed onto his white shirt and made a dreadful stain. I began to shake, and sobbed out: "That was not fair."

"Oh—my darling—I am a brute,—I own it—" he said, in an agony of contrition, and reached for his handkerchief.

But I sobbed harder than ever, and when he asked what he had done, how he had offended me to such a degree, I sobbed: "Ink won't come out. It won't! It won't!"

At that point Molly put her head suspiciously round the door, and when she saw me gulping and sobbing into Mr Prynne-Edwards' handkerchief, she gave him a look like a gimlet. He looked bewildered, poor man, as well he might.

"I have just asked her to marry me," he said helplessly.

Well, Molly sorted everything out, sat me firmly in the chair and showed him the door—very nicely, for she thinks he is ever such a nice gentleman. He turned at the door, and said to me, quietly, but with such a sense of purpose I can't describe it: "I will come back."

And then he went, and I have come to sit in the White Room to sort out the tumbled pieces of the morning and put them in order.

March 20th

I have decided what to give Father for his birthday. A gold seal for his watch-chain, with some of my hair inside it. I am going to send Robert to town tomorrow to purchase the seal and take a lock of my hair for the man to put inside.

Sundays here always depend a great deal on the weather. If the weather is gloomy, the predominant feeling is one of Methodist fervour, which I find excessively dull and depressing. If the weather is fair, then I find Sundays cheerful—and today is fair, so a fig for Molly's admonitions about proper behaviour for the Lord's Day.

I put on my cloak and came out with Mr Rochester to walk in the garden. We have been wandering in the orchard, and down to the kitchen garden. I have been thinking about all sorts of things—especially what happened yesterday.

How difficult life is. I cannot help myself from liking Mr Prynne-Edwards, simply because he so obviously cares for me. But liking is not the same as loving, and I do not want to love him because it would mean the end of my peaceful life here. And yet, it seems he is willing to love me, although I will bring him problems too—his family will see to that. Then he is braver than I am. Or am I simply more sensible?

I wish Father would come home. I had never realised until he went away, just how fond I am of Father.

March 21st

I am sitting in the library, feeling as shattered as if I had been through the mangle, but triumphant as well. We have just had a visit from Clarissa Prynne-Edwards and her mama, and they have driven off in high dudgeon.

To start at the beginning, after breakfast I sent Robert into town with instructions about the gold seal for Father's birthday, and I was just handing him the lock of my hair, carefully folded in soft paper, which is to go inside the seal, when there was a terrible commotion in the Dome Room, a thunderous knocking as though someone was trying to break down the front door. It was Miss Prynne-Edwards and her mama.

"They said to tell you they've called, Miss Sophy," said Robert, coming back from the front door.

I was quite startled, as you can imagine, and hastily smoothed my hair and dress, then went up the steps to the Dome Room. The front doors were open, and framed in the arch of the doorway, I could see an elegant carriage with Mrs Prynne-Edwards' imperious face peering out. I caught a glimpse of Clarissa beyond, with her yellow curls pulled back under a bonnet of tawny velvet. She was frowning and quite spoiling all her prettiness.

"Mrs Prynne-Edwards—Miss Prynne-Edwards—what a pleasant surprise," I said. "Won't you come in?"

At this, Mr Prynne-Edwards' mama fanned herself with a little lace handkerchief, and said in a far-away voice: "Oh! Clarissa, I feel faint."

"Nonsense, Mama," said Clarissa, supporting her while she darted a venomous look at me. I remembered all the nasty things she had said the last time she came, riding alone, and I stiffened my spine and met her look calmly.

"You know you wanted to come," Clarissa went on. "To talk to Miss—Miss Roy."

"Yes! Oh dear, I wish Harry had been home," said Mrs Prynne-Edwards, and she got out of the carriage with a great rustling of silk petticoats and smoothing of skirts, with the groom standing by to help her. Clarissa clambered out after her, looking more elegant than ever in a tawny gown with the very latest sleeves, and with her hands in a little sable muff.

I led them into the house.

"If you'll come with me," I said. At the end of the Dome Room, I could see Mair and Shan and Molly, all eagerly watching, and I ordered: "Molly, some tea in the library, if you please."

"The library!" said Mrs Prynne-Edwards, sounding scandalised.

"I am afraid we live very simply," I answered. I was beginning to feel angry at her tone. "The library is the only room with a fire. But if you prefer, you can sit in the kitchen instead."

"Oh! Clarissa!" moaned Mrs Prynne-Edwards, looking at me as though she feared I might bite her.

"Here, Mama," said Clarissa, solicitously taking her mother's elbow, and they followed me through the Dome Room and down the steps into the hall, and into the library. The fire was crackling brightly.

I asked if they would like to sit down. Mrs Prynne-Edwards did so, after nearly tripping over poor Mr Rochester, who, amazed at this invasion of his sanctum, had crept under the chair. He yelped with pain, and I picked him up and stood waiting for them to approach the subject of their visit.

After a moment, Mama, having stared at me in between fanning herself with her lace handkerchief, said: "Dick told us—last night—that he means to marry you."

Well, I was so furious at this, both because of the way she was staring at me, and also because Mr Prynne-Edwards had, as I felt, betrayed a trust in gossiping about me when nothing was settled, that I did not answer, as I should have done, that he might say what he liked, I had no intention of marrying him. Instead, I said, with an imp of mischief prompting my words: "Yes, I believe he does."

"But—the thing's impossible," she wailed, staring at me in dismay.

"Not at all," I answered very demurely, with cold anger seething inside. "I am sure Father won't stand in my way."

"Oh!" said Mama, shutting her eyes and leaning back against the chair.

Clarissa, who was standing behind her mother as though to protect her, suddenly leaned forward. "You schemed to get him—you—you hussy," she hissed. "But you shan't have him. Mama, tell her."

"My husband will never allow such a match," says Mama. "He is away at present but—oh, dear! Clarissa, I feel quite ill."

By this time, I was so furious that I was beginning to shake with rage. I held Mr Rochester tighter and said in a very quiet voice: "I believe Mr Prynne-Edwards is old enough to choose for himself without the help of his family."

Clarissa looked at me with such dislike that I felt ill myself, but Mrs Prynne-Edwards leaned forward.

"My dear," she said. "Be reasonable. Even you must see the disgrace such a match would bring on the family. Dick could have anybody—and for him to marry you—."

She looked at me so pointedly that I felt myself going scarlet red, but with anger not embarrassment.

"It would be disastrous—quite disastrous!" she said, fanning herself very rapidly. "We can't allow it. The very idea of Dick—marrying a bride in such a condition—"

"Damaged goods," hissed Clarissa.

"Perhaps," I said sweetly, "He would like to wait until after the baby is born and marry me then."

Mrs Prynne-Edwards gasped "Oh!" at that, and proceeded to faint, while Clarissa fussed round her with smelling-salts, and Mr Rochester whined.

I waited until she had recovered herself, then said clearly: "Mr Prynne-Edwards has asked me to marry him—but whether or not I have accepted is his business and mine. But if I had, let me tell you, ma'am, I would marry him gladly, whatever obstacles you or your husband might try to put in my way."

"Never!" moaned Mrs Prynne-Edwards, getting to her feet, and panting with outrage. "Let us go, Clarissa, from this barbarous house. I must summon Harry home at once. This is too much for me to cope with alone! Oh! I shall have one of my attacks, I can feel it coming on—."

"When Papa comes home, then we'll see," said Clarissa, as she assisted her mother to the door. They rustled out, a hatchet-faced Molly showing them the way, leaving Mr Rochester and me standing on the library carpet, victors of the field—for the moment anyway.

March 22nd

Father is coming home tomorrow. We have had a letter ordering Robert to meet the train, such a mysterious letter, as though Father has some great news to tell us when he arrives.

I am beginning to feel as though he might have been just the sort of man that Miss Brontë's Mr Rochester was. He loved my mother and married her even though she was practically penniless, just like Jane Eyre, except that my mother had been brought up as a lady, even though her father hadn't much money. I have begun to understand lately just how much he loved her, and why he was so odd and strange after she died.

The weather today is very threatening, and we are all jumpy. It is thundery weather, with a strange stillness over everything. The park and valley are brooding quietly under a horrible yellow light. I wish the storm would come. There is something cleansing and good about storms, they clear the air and sweep the cobwebs away. I feel just in the mood for a good loud one—to sweep away the nastiness of yesterday's visit.

The nursery suite is finished now. I went up after luncheon when Mair came in to tell me that the workmen had finished. She looked a bit like a blushing peony with her red hair and red face. Any attention from Gwilym reduces her almost to gibbering imbecility.

I thanked the workmen pleasantly, and they have just gone, taking their tools and bits and pieces with them. Mair is desolate, but I told her to cheer up, as there are other fish in the sea.

"Yes, miss," she said, without enthusiasm. Then she added, all in a rush: "But he was such a lovely singer, miss, and so handsome, and got a real way with him."

Molly sniffed at that, and told her that it was the ones that had a way with them that you had to watch out for most.

Did I remember to say that I sent Robert into town yesterday with the lock of my hair and the order for Father's birthday seal, and it will be ready in a few days? His birthday is this day week.

March 23rd

The threatened thunderstorm broke last night while we were all in bed. The air had been quite oppressive yesterday evening, and Molly had a headache, and when we were all asleep—at about one o'clock in the morning there was a terrible crash and bang, and then lightning flickering so that I could see the yard and the stables and everything quite clearly.

That started us off! A scream from Mair and a screech from Shan, who is still not used to being on her own—she has six brothers and sisters at home, and they all sleep in the same room—and there was Mr Rochester whining and pushing himself under the bedclothes with me, his little body shivering.

Molly and Mair and Shan got up while the storm was going on and sat in the kitchen with the curtains shut, but I decided to stay warm in bed, with Mr Rochester huddled up against me, and watch the storm through the window. Some of the cracks were so loud, directly overhead, that one would have thought the world would split in pieces with the sound. Afterwards, I went to sleep with the rain beating on the stable roof, and woke to a lovely fresh morning and the knowledge that Father is coming home today. Robert has taken the carriage, driving off proudly through the puddles in the yard, and along the drive, to meet Father's train.

I think I can hear voices, and the sound of wheels, earlier than we expected. Yes—it's Father!

March 24th

Such an amazing thing has happened that I can hardly write about it. Father has brought a lady home with him! Her name is Miss Fortescue, and she is the sister of the friend that Father went to see. Her other name is Hélène—it is spelt like that because her mother was French.

To start at the beginning, when we heard the carriage coming into the yard yesterday, we all went to the door—Molly and Mair and Shan too, and there was Father handing a lady out of the carriage, and Robert looking so amazed that I thought it was a wonder he had managed to get them home safely.

"Sophy," cried Father, when he saw me. "My dear child." And he gave me a great hug, and then turned to the lady, who was standing in the yard waiting to be introduced.

"This is my daughter Sophy," he said. And to me: "I want you to meet Hélène—"

Then he looked up at the faces peering out of the door, Molly and Mair and Shan, all looking flabbergasted, and growled: "I can't talk to you with an audience. Let's go in."

"Yes, Father," I said, asking uncertainly, for I was just as amazed as everyone else: "Will Miss—?"

"Miss Fortescue, but please, won't you call me Hélène?" said the lady, speaking for the first time. She has a delightful voice, the sort I like, very soft and low, but clear.

"Will you be staying?" I asked her.

"Don't be rude, Sophy," growled Father, very touchily.

"I'm not," I said. "But if Miss—Hélène is staying, Molly and the girls will have to get a room ready. We were not expecting a visitor."

She put her gloved hand lightly on my arm and smiled at me.

"If you will have me," she said. "I hope to stay for a few days, that is all."

Father stalked on ahead of us into the house. Even then, I should have realized that he was so touchy because he wanted me to like Hélène.

We went into the house, and I told Molly that the lady would be staying, and for them to get a room ready—the big painted bedroom that used to be my mother's is the best, so I said they could do that one.

"It's rabbit pie for supper," she said, glowering.

I said that would be all right. The lady would understand that we hadn't been expecting anyone.

Then, full of amazement, as though I was walking in a dream, I went into the library, where Father and Miss Fortescue had gone. They were standing before the fire, she exclaiming over the room. They looked round as I entered.

"Come in, Sophy," said Father. He cleared his throat and began: "This is something of a surprise for you, I expect."

Then Hélène touched his arm.

"Let me explain, John," she said, and came forward to me.

"Your Father met me the day before yesterday, Sophy," she said in that lovely low voice. "At my brother's. He was all ready to leave London, but when we saw each other—" She stopped and looked at Father, and it was as though a golden light shone from her eyes, and from Father's.

"He has asked me to marry him," said Hélène, quietly. "I have accepted. But we had no time to arrange anything—I came up with him to—to meet you—and to see his home—"

They waited, both looking like naughty children, to see what I would do. I have never seen Father look like that before, just like a little boy, waiting to know if he will be punished. As for Hélène, with her beautiful voice and soft grave eyes, and her gown that smelled of lavender, I loved her so much that it was all I could do not to throw myself into her arms and hug her. But the thought of Father bowled over by a chance meeting in London, and asking her to marry him, when he had been lonely for so many years, and wandering in all weathers on the Dyke, and all his shirts worn to threads, and his hair going grey, and his face so lined and tired—it all caught in my throat and came out in a sob.

Instantly, Hélène was full of concern.

"We should have told her more gently," she exclaimed.

"No," I sobbed, and then somehow, her arm was round me, and so was Father's, and we were all sobbing and laughing together, and Mr Rochester was whining and pushing at my ankles.

"I think it's—so beautiful," I gulped. "I'm so glad for you, Father—and so happy."

Hélène was crying too, with tears trembling on her lashes, and shining like dew in the morning on a wild rose.

"I was afraid you might not want me," she said. "You've had him to yourself all these years—" and she laughed through her tears. "To think of being afraid—of you, Sophy. Oh, I can hardly believe it, John—I feel as though I've come home, really home."

March 25th

I didn't have much time to write in my diary yesterday, what with one thing and another, and I have hardly begun to put on paper the excitement at Hélène's arrival, and the shaking-up that we have all had. But this morning, Father and Hélène have gone for a walk on the Dyke, and Molly is in command in the kitchen. I am sitting in the drawing-room (where a bright fire is burning in Hélène's honour) and have a good hour or so to myself in which to continue the story.

Molly has been scrupulously polite, and as for the girls, they think Miss Fortescue is next only to the Queen in magnificence, and they are tongue-tied in her presence. But she has been so charming to them that they are ready to die for her. I think Molly is jealous.

"Coming away like that, with a gentleman she'd only just met," she grumbled to herself, when I was in the kitchen. "Lady-like behaviour, indeed!"

I said nothing. I have not had time yet to sort out my own thoughts, but I am happy beyond words that they met each other. Hélène is not like Clarissa and Mrs Prynne-Edwards and the society ladies I have known. Her brother, the one that was in school with Father, is a very successful London publisher, and their family is very well thought of in London society. Their mother was the daughter of a French aristocrat who went to the Guillotine during the Revolution, so Hélène was telling me yesterday. It is all very romantic.

She is not young, she is about thirty-two, and very intelligent and educated. She has been to all sorts of interesting places, Italy and France and Switzerland, with her brother, and she can speak French and Italian as well as English.

But the thing that has endeared me most towards her is the fact that she fits in so beautifully with the house. I could tell right from when I first saw her stepping out of the carriage on Father's arm, that she belongs here as we do—a most amazing thing.

She has slept in the big painted bedroom, which the girls and Molly hastily prepared on the day they arrived, and yesterday morning, I was up early to make sure she had everything she wanted, hot water for a bath and breakfast in bed, hot rolls and coffee and a fresh egg from the farm.

It was a lovely morning, and the sunlight was pouring in through the windows which face over the park. She was sitting up in a rose-coloured velvet wrapper when I went in with her breakfast, and her soft hair was tied on her shoulders with a ribbon, and she looked very young—younger even than me.

"Sophy—my dear, you shouldn't have. There's no need to wait on me like a servant," she said, when she saw the tray.

"I don't mind," I said, and smiled at her.

She invited me to sit with her and share her breakfast, so I did, and we talked, about all sorts of things. It is amazing, but even though I have only known her for a day, I feel as though it has been for years.

She told me about her meeting with Father. Her brother had given her the manuscript of Father's book to read, and she wanted to meet the author. I forgot to mention, in all the excitement, that Father's friend is going to publish it, and he thinks it is a magnificent book. ("It will be the definitive work," he said).

"Your father is a great man, Sophy," said Hélène, and she went on to tell me how, the day they were introduced, Father asked her to marry him, about half an hour after they met, in the conservatory of Mr Fortescue's house, and she answered "Yes" without any hesitation at all. And the next day, when he asked her to come home for a visit, she merely nodded and sent for her things in order to be able to catch the train with him.

It sounds just like a novel, just like Thomas Kyffin's Spanish wife following him across the world. She is going to stay until after Father's birthday, and they are to be married as soon as possible, but very quietly.

"I can hardly believe it—I am afraid I shall wake up," she said, and laughed. "I had thought I would never marry—but I am so happy, it was worth waiting for this."

I cannot help wondering what Mrs Prynne-Edwards and all the county here will say, when the news gets round. Hélène is a person they can hardly disapprove of, she has been to Windsor and actually spoken to people like Mr Thackeray and Mrs Gaskell and Miss Brontë. (They have brought me one of her books, *Villette*.) Also, she has a lot of money of her own, and her clothes are so indescribably handsome, she says they have come from Paris. She will put Clarissa and Mrs Prynne-Edwards and Christina Hurst quite in the shade.

March 26th

Yesterday I showed Hélène the gardens, and over the house. Father was going to come too, but at the last moment Mr Turner arrived from town, and Father had to stay to go over the estate business with him. It was so funny. Mr Turner had come in with the usual gentlemanly leer on his face (intended for me) but when he saw Hélène standing in the hall, his jaw dropped and he looked as though he was going to turn and run.

"Hah! Turner," said Father. "Hélène, this is Mr Turner, my estate manager. May I present the future Lady Roy—Miss Fortescue."

Hélène put out her hand to him with a smile. This was the moment for one of Mr Turner's would-be-gallant speeches, but his voice had deserted him. He stuttered and stammered like a boy, and then Father rescued him and took him into the study.

We went down the steps into the garden. Hélène loves the gardens and the house already. I told her the story of Sir Thomas Kyffin building it, and his Spanish wife, and her face lit up.

"What a lovely tale," she said.

But when we were talking in the orchard, she grew more thoughtful.

"I don't want you to think of me as a step-mother, Sophy," she said gravely, looking at me. "Do you think you might be able to regard me as an older sister?"

"I have always wanted a sister," I said. And then, what with one thing and another, I felt to my dismay, a sob rising in my throat.

I know what had caused it. It was because I had seen them come in from their walk on the Dyke, laughing and with bright faces, and Hélène turned to Father, saying something, and he looked at her and the words died on her lips, and I saw such an expression come to her face that my heart began to beat very hard, and I thought of when Mr Prynne-Edwards kissed me in the library, and I felt so desolate all at once, that I hurried on up the stairs (I was on the landing at the turn) before they could speak to me.

It carried on all through luncheon, like a great heavy stone in my chest, growing heavier all the time. I wanted to cry, and I was angry with myself, and I felt so full of misery that I just wanted to go and lie on my bed and sob. But all that happened was that when we were in the orchard and I saw the fruit trees with the blossom trembling on them, and I thought of the first time he said he loved me, I felt more miserable than ever, and I gave a sort of gulp.

Hélène looked so sympathetic, but didn't ask any questions, that in a moment, we were pacing arm-in-arm under the blossom along the walks, and I told her all about Charles and the baby. She listened very quietly, without interrupting, and when I was finished, she still said nothing, but pressed my arm.

I began to regret it as soon as I had told her.

"I suppose you'll say I deserve it all, because I didn't behave like a lady," I said bitterly, and I gave one of the clumps of crocus a kick.

"Do you really want to know what I think?" she asked, and when I turned round unwillingly to look, I found she was smiling. "Your father was right. He told me on the train that he had a daughter he would not exchange for a hundred young ladies." Suddenly she leaned forward and took my hands. "Darling Sophy. There's no need to bristle so, just like a hedgehog. You are very loveable, you know."

"But how can you tell—if you are really in love?" I said before I could think. "You love Father. But how did you know that he was the person you wanted to marry? How did you not—do what I did? I regret it now, not the baby, but Charles and everything. But I didn't realise, at the time. I thought he meant it when he said he loved me—and now, it has ruined my whole future." I hid my face in my hands ashamed to look at her, both because of what she might think and also because of what I was saying. I hadn't even realized that I had such thoughts, they spilled out from the inside of my mind like water bubbling up from the earth, without my own volition.

Hélène took my hands gently, and pulled them away from my face.

"Your future is what you make it yourself, Sophy," she said, and looking into her calm, grave eyes, I knew she was right. She is so wise—I wish I had met her years ago. She smiled, then, very encouragingly, and her face dimpled. "As for knowing whether you are in love, the thing to do is to ask yourself, not, 'Does he really love me?' but 'Do I really love him?' "

I have been thinking about it and it is true. If Charles had not insisted so loudly that he loved me, I would never have thought of going away with him for a minute.

March 27th

The time has passed so enjoyably since Hélène arrived that I had almost forgotten about Father's watch-seal, but yesterday, Father went to town with Hélène in the carriage, and I let her into the secret and she smuggled the package back from the jeweller's for me without Father suspecting anything. She has bought him a set of books, all magnificently bound in calf with the titles in gold. The works of some Latin authors, I forget which. Father has already got lots of books in his library, of course, but Hélène held up one of the new set with a smile, very mischievous, when I told her.

"He hasn't the poems of Catullus—I've asked," she said.

We have been spending our time merrily: I have played for them in the evening, with the drawing-room brightly lit, and Hélène applauded my singing. We have also gone over the house, and Hélène has all sorts of plans.

"Shall you mind, Sophy?" she asked, laughing. I told her that I would not, and described how the house looked when we had my ball, with everything shining and the scent of the flowers drifting and the dresses and jewels.

She came with me to see the nursery suite, and admired the new wallpaper. They hope to be married long before June—in a few weeks, I think—so she will be here with me when the baby is born.

"I'm glad," I said shyly. It seems strange to have someone else to depend on, and I am not really afraid, but in the privacy of my diary, I can admit that it will be a comfort to cling to Hélène's hand if the pain is very bad.

Molly has been very polite still, very cool and correct. She has withdrawn into the kitchen, which she says is her "rightful place," whatever that means. I went to talk to her when Father and Hélène were out in town yesterday with Robert.

Mair and Shan were bubbling over with excitement. They have never seen such thrilling events in their whole lives before, nor been in contact with a lady like Hélène.

"Her gowns, miss, ooh, lovely they are," said Mair, with a sigh of delight.

"And lace all over her chemises, and ribbon," breathed Shan almost reverently.

"Oh, she's a fine lady all right," said Molly, but very reluctantly.

"You do like her, Molly, don't you?" I asked.

"It's not my place to say anything Miss Sophy," she said, shutting her mouth with a snap.

And that was all I could get out of her. It seems strange for Molly to be keeping her opinions to herself. I hope she will not be miserable, but I suspect, from the look in her eye, that she is enjoying her self-imposed martyrdom in the kitchen. She also knows that she is safe enough. Hélène has commented already what an excellent cook she is, and it would break Father's heart to send her away.

They came back from town full of laughter at the reception they had received. The news of Hélène's arrival has gone buzzing round the county like a heath-fire on the hills, sweeping all before it. And I am sure that society is stunned to see how elegant and lovely she is.

Father had taken her to town to buy her a ring for their engagement. Hélène did not mind whether she had a ring or not, but Father insisted. She showed it to me when they came back, glittering on her finger, opals sparkling all the colours of the rainbow in their milky depths.

"Opals—but they are unlucky!" I exclaimed before I could stop myself.

"Not for me," she said, with a smile. "They are for such unbelievable happiness, I can't believe it even now." She touched the ring gently, and her face was very soft. "They are so lovely, they will remind me of it, always."

There was a surprise for me, too. Father came into the library where I was writing, while Hélène was taking off her cloak and unloading her parcels. He had brought a large box with him. He didn't even wait to take off his greatcoat, but thrust the box into my hands.

It was very heavy, and there was a key to open it, but it was in the lock, so I turned it and lifted the lid. It was full of jewellery, all old and tarnished and in need of a good clean, but still the stones caught the light from the fire and splintered it into the most wonderful sparks of colour.

I caught my breath in amazement, and Father looked pleased.

"Like 'em, eh?" he said. "Well, they're yours now. It's time a pretty girl wore them again. They've been locked in that safe for too long."

Suddenly I knew what he meant, and I asked: "Were they—my mother's?"

But I knew the answer, even before he nodded. He picked up one piece, a bracelet of filigree set with pearls and some blue stones that I think are turquoise, and his voice was very quiet.

"I gave her the set—on our wedding day," he said, and then he laid it down gently, and turned and went out of the library. I heard him going across the hall to his study.

I looked for the rest of the set. There is a parure in the same pearls and turquoises with the filigree fine and delicate and fragile. There are some other things too, rings and pins and a necklace of moonstones. I have not looked at all of them. I sat with the box on my knees and in a few moments, Hélène came in and I could hear Molly going across the hall and the clinking of tea-cups.

This morning, I had forgotten about the jewels, until I saw the box standing on the tall-boy in my bedroom, reflecting the bright light from outside. I opened it and lifted out the pearl bracelet and its matching necklace, ear-rings and brooch. I have never had any jewellery before, and never felt the lack, but for my mother's sake, I will treasure them.

March 28th

I have wrapped up my present for Father this morning. The jeweller has done it very nicely, the gold seal looks most impressive, and they have plaited the lock of hair into a pattern, and it looks very artistic. Hélène says I have beautiful hair, she saw me brushing it one morning and she exclaimed over its gloss and thickness.

She has taken Father out for another walk this morning so that Molly and I can get on with all our secret plans for his birthday tomorrow. What a birthday it will be! The house is humming with excitement already, it will be the best birthday celebration we have had for years.

Molly was a bit more friendly when I went to help her in the kitchen. She has been sewing and knitting busily, and this morning she showed me the beautiful white fleecy shawl for the baby, which she has finished. I exclaimed over it, it is a lovely thing, and the baby will love it, I am sure.

"Not as much as the fine things her ladyship'll give it," she said bitterly.

"Molly! What a thing to say," I exclaimed in real anger. "Her coming has made no difference to the fact that you belong here too. You always have, and you always will." I put my arms round her. "Where would we be without you?"

She looked a bit more cheered at that, and said she supposed she'd better be getting on with the cake, and how was I expecting her to manage everything, and be a lady's maid to visitors and all, she didn't know.

Later

Father and Hélène came in just then, so I put my diary away and talked to them. They were discussing Father's book. Hélène is fascinated by the Dyke, she thinks it is a chapter of history right on our doorstep, and she has spent a long time looking at the things Father has found, which are labelled and displayed in the study.

"You will be famous when the book comes out John," she said to Father. "You wait and see."

I was thrilled, and was going to ask her some more about it, but just then, Mair came to tell us luncheon was ready, and after luncheon, Doctor Hawk called. "The news has spread, of course," he said, as he bowed over Hélène's hand. "The county can talk of nothing else." He twinkled at her. "They seem to feel I have neglected my duty in not coming to report immediately on your exact colour of hair and eyes and style of dress. "He came into the drawing-room to examine me, and when the door was shut behind Molly, whom he sent on another of his contrived errands so that he could talk to me in private, he said: "Well? And what do you think about all this, Sophy? It's not upsetting you is it? Though it's been rather a shock, I imagine."

I told him that I was delighted at the news, and that it hadn't upset me a bit. He looked at me very hard as I spoke, and then nodded, as though he was satisfied.

"At least this will put a stop to the gossip you dislike so

much," he said, with a smile. "Your father has stolen the limelight now, with a vengeance."

After he had gone, I had a wonderful idea and I could hardly wait to find Father and Hélène and tell them.

"I think you should get married in the chapel," I said, when I rushed into the big painted bedroom, which they were in the process of discussing. It is the master bedroom, and will be theirs when they marry.

"The chapel!" said Father, and I could tell the idea appealed to him. Hélène looked mystified and said: "Which chapel, Sophy?"

"The private chapel, the one that belongs to the house," I said breathlessly, and I took Hélène to see it. Father came too, bringing the key from his study, and he unlocked the door and we all went inside. It smelt a bit musty, but the floor was quite dry. Hélène was enchanted. She exclaimed with delight over the slit window and the smallness of it and the carved figures round the walls and the groined roof.

"In the morning, the sun comes through the window, it faces east," I said. "And we could have lots of flowers." I told her that the chapel had been built for Thomas Kyffin's Spanish bride, and she was delighted.

"I couldn't possibly think of being married anywhere else," she said to Father, and he promised to arrange it. I felt so excited, I thought I would burst. I will fill the chapel with flowers until it looks unrecognisable. We will have to get more of the girls in to help, for no doubt Hélène's family will be coming from London, and her famous brother, and they will want to stay here at least for a day or so. I can hardly wait to get on with the arrangements. It is far more thrilling than the dinner party.

March 29th

Everyone else has gone to bed but I wanted to sit up and write about today in my diary. The fire is burning low, the house is full of comfortable warmth and the echoes of our festivities, and Mr Rochester is snuffling against my feet.

What a day it has been! It started with us all giving our gifts to Father this morning at breakfast. He was so amazed—I think he had quite forgotten that it was his birthday, his mind has been so occupied with thoughts of Hélène—she is going back to London tomorrow, and I will miss her terribly, so I can understand how Father must feel.

His face was a picture as he stared at the packages, with Molly beaming from the sideboard, and Hélène looking like a little girl, so eager, on the other side of the table, and Mair and Shan peering round the door.

"What's this?" said Father.

"Birthday presents, of course," I answered, and got up and hugged him. "Happy birthday, Father. Had you forgotten?"

"Hah!" he snorted, like a schoolboy caught out, and he opened the packages.

Molly had rallied to the occasion and given him a muffler, knitted by herself. It is in chocolate brown. Father's eyebrows leaped when he saw it but he thanked her gravely, and she beamed with pride. Robert had supplied a bunch of flowers to give a festive note (they are our flowers really, I suppose, but Robert was very anxious to be included, so Father duly admired them, but his mouth twitched). Then he opened the watch seal from me, and the sunlight caught it, and made it glitter like yellow fire.

"What?" he said, examining it.

"It's for your watch chain, Father," I hastened to explain. "And it has a lock of my hair inside it to make sure that you think about me every time you seal a letter."

He looked at me with such a loving look and a twinkle in his eyes, that I felt my throat going all stiff, and he said: "No fear of my forgetting you, Sophy."

Then Father took the paper off Hélène's present, and there was the lovely calf-bound volume of Catullus' poems. He insisted on opening it there and then, and reading aloud some of the poems to us, which he did, while Hélène blushed and laughed.

They were in Latin, of course, and nobody could understand them, which was fortunate, as they are very shocking, but Molly and Shan and Mair listened admiringly as Father declaimed, and Hélène protested that he shouldn't read them aloud.

"Nobody'll be able to make head or tail of them—except Sophy, she's done a little Latin," said Father. He put down the book, and gave her a look which reminded me of when I saw them coming in from the Dyke, and said softly: "Food for the soul, indeed."

Hélène met the look and said that she was glad he liked it, but what about some food for the body too, and we all ended up laughing and Molly served up the breakfast, and we had a lovely merry meal.

After breakfast, we all went for a walk. Hélène and I took an arm each of Father's and we walked a long way in the park, and right up to the bluebell wood, with the fresh wind scudding the clouds across the sky, and the valley all spread out bright and shining below us. We stopped to point out landmarks to Hélène. The church tower in town, like a finger raised to heaven, and I told her that there is a tale that the flagstones of our terrace are exactly the same height as the top of the church tower.

"And there's a legend—I'm putting it in my history of the house—," I said, "that a secret passage runs from the house to somewhere, no-one seems to know where."

Hélène was thrilled, and asked me lots of questions about the house's history.

When we came back, it was time for luncheon and we had large appetites because of our walk in the fresh air. I rested in the library afterwards and I really was quite tired after the walk, so I didn't write in my diary. In any case, the most important part of the day was to come. We made a big occasion of dinner, with all of us changing into formal clothes. I put on my green velvet dinner dress, which fortunately still fits, and Hélène wore a lovely dress of a soft rose colour, with flounces trimmed in darker rose, and she did her hair with some little bits of lace and rose flowers, and looked so lovely when she came down that I wanted to cry. Father looked so proud, and I really felt as though we were a real family, with all of us sitting in the soft candle-light and Molly, our faithful retainer waiting on us, and Mair and Shan wearing their best expressions along with their caps and aprons, flitting in and out.

It was a lovely ending to the day, but so sad in a way. Tomorrow, Father is taking Hélène to catch the train back to London, and I will miss her so much. Also, I have not heard anything from Mr Prynne-Edwards. Has he forgotten me? I have not had very much time to think about him while Hélène was here, but the evening, with all the shadows of the dark house closing round me, is a time when forbidden thoughts come creeping in, like ghosts and I feel a sort of pain in my heart, I do not know why.

The fire is burning so low that a chill is beginning to come into the room and Mr Rochester is twitching in his sleep, snapping at some imaginary thing that is bothering him. The house is all around me, like a brooding guardian monster. But still I have this pain in my heart.

PART FOUR

April 6th

The rain is pouring down in torrents, but very light, fine rain, with the sun trying to come out. I have come to the White Room to sit in the reflected light and glimmer, it is almost like being under water, with a green and silver glitter moving on the white walls and ceiling.

Such a lot of things have happened since Hélène went back to London, we have been feverishly preparing for the wedding, which is very soon, in just over a week, on the 15th, and Father has had some proofs of his book to read and correct. The publisher wants to publish it as soon as possible.

I have to catch up with all the news because on the morning when Father was taking Hélène to the train, I caught my foot in one of the rugs and fell, and sprained my wrist. It was quite painful and I could not write or use my hand for several days.

Hélène said, when she went, that she would send me some specially nice things to wear, and she did. Yesterday a parcel arrived and there were two lovely *robes-de-chambre* in it, and a magnificent shawl in shades of green and gold, with a thick fringe. The dresses are beautiful, I have never seen clothes so fine. There was also a third dress, which I am keeping to wear for the wedding, it is a pale green, trimmed with blond lace and dark green ribbons, and it goes beautifully with the shawl. I think I shall look presentable for the wedding, which is very important, as I am to be Hélène's bridesmaid.

It will be only a small affair; it seems that Hélène's father is dead and her mother (the one who escaped from France during the Revolution) is an invalid and does not go out, so only her brother will be coming.

The Bishop is going to marry them, and Father has consulted

the Vicar from the village, who will assist. He is a quiet little man, who is dazed at the idea of Sir John marrying a London lady in the chapel that has never been used for years, I think he thinks the whole thing is not really in order, and he would be much happier if Father would agree to be married in his church, or even in the cathedral, which is where all the big fashionable weddings are held.

Father told me the other day that if I marry, I shall have a very handsome dowry settled on me. I suppose I am an heiress, but the thought doesn't make any difference. I feel exactly the same as I did before.

"Thank you Father," I said. "But I don't think I shall be marrying anybody." I managed to speak calmly, although I have shed a tear or two during the last week, much to my chagrin, because there has still been no word from Mr Prynne-Edwards.

Father twinkled at me and told me I sounded like a Greek tragedy. But it is difficult to maintain a tragic attitude to life when everywhere is so bright and vivid and bursting into blossom.

Hélène has written to me, and told me about her wedding dress, which is being made at a famous Paris fashion house, at great expense and in a great hurry. It sounds lovely.

"It is very simple," she wrote. "Cream-coloured silk, embroidered with true lovers-knots."

I feel quite grown-up and indulgent about their romance. Now that I will never have one of my own, it is sweet in a way to see a romance unfolding before my eyes, although there is something of pain in it too. But I don't want to spoil Father's pleasure, although I shall cry when Hélène comes down in her beautiful Paris dress and with her veil hanging down her back (the veil is an heirloom, it belongs to her father's family, and it is almost priceless) and holding her bouquet.

April 7th

Molly and the girls are hard at work cleaning and sweeping, dusting and polishing. The big painted bedroom is all ready, with the posters of the great bed polished and shining with beeswax, and every corner sparkling. On their wedding day, I will put flowers in the room, white bridal flowers to fill it with scent.

How lovely to see this room happy again! There has always been a sort of melancholy air here ever since my mother died, but all that is swept away now, along with the cobwebs, and the best patchwork quilt, which is very old, has been brought out of the cupboard where Molly has guarded it jealously, like the Golden Fleece, and it makes a rich pool of colour on the bed.

I wondered whether Father and Hélène would want to go away after the wedding, to Italy perhaps. They are both wealthy enough to afford an extravagant honeymoon, but they have decided they would rather stay here instead, quietly, at home. Part of the reason, I am sure, is that they do not want to leave me alone just now. Hélène smiled at me when she was telling me about it, and added: "We will travel later in the year—all of us, Sophy." How considerate she is.

I could not think what to give them for a wedding present. I have racked my brains, consulted with Molly, and in the end decided to give them a set of Waterford glass and a crystal decanter, just a gift for show, really, because I am also going to present them with my history of the house, when that is finished, but it will not be ready in time.

I have resigned myself to a life of self-abnegation here at home, and perhaps, in order to pass the time, I will continue to write. I will become a famous authoress, and when people ask why I never married, I will say: "I am dedicated to my work."

It is a good thing Father can't read this. He would laugh. But really, I cannot see that there is any more dignified way of life open to me, not after Mr Prynne-Edwards' desertion. I must admit—but only very privately—that he has hurt me very much. I had thought better of him, I had thought he was honest and brave and meant all the things he said. But I suppose when his Papa came home, and told him he must never see me again, he agreed to do what his Papa said. He is just like Charles, just like all men except Father. They are such cowards.

April 8th

It is no wonder that I have not heard from Mr Prynne-Edwards. We have had news today from Doctor Hawk, who called ostensibly to see my wrist, but I think he really wanted to tell me what had been happening at the Works.

It is most exciting, Molly and the girls have been chattering all day in the kitchen, all about it. It seems that Mr Prynne-Edwards, that is, our Mr Prynne-Edwards' papa, is a partner in the business, or was, rather, because for some reason which I can't imagine, and which Doctor Hawk didn't explain, it was necessary for one of them to sell out to the other—the question was, which? Because both of them, Mr Prynne-Edwards and Mr Roberts, wanted to buy the other out.

"So they decided to settle it with a race," said Doctor Hawk, with his fastidious nose wrinkling slightly. "It was Harry Prynne-Edwards' idea, I gather. Anyway, it was all settled—they were to race on horseback from the gates of Pengwern to the Works, and whoever got there first was to buy the other out."

"How exciting!" I burst out, clasping my hands. But I was a

bit apprehensive because I was afraid Mr Prynne-Edwards might have lost the race. Doctor Hawk shook his head, smiling as he saw my face.

"You're too transparent, child," he said. Then he went on and told me that at the time when the race took place—it was yesterday afternoon—crowds of workers from the Works gathered and lots of people from town, to watch. Some of them were betting on who would win. And then the two men arrived, with their horses, all ready for the race.

"Well, they mounted, and old Gwynne shot off a pistol in the air, and they were off," said Doctor Hawk. "The crowds were cheering and shouting, and the two of them galloped off, riding like the devil—forgive me, Sophy—to get to the Works first."

"Oh! And who won?" I gasped.

"Prynne-Edwards, of course," said Doctor Hawk. "He was the men's choice. They barricaded all the gates into the Works, and wouldn't let Roberts through. So Prynne-Edwards rode in triumphantly through rows of cheering men. And that was it."

"Oh! I am glad," I said, thinking how relieved Mr Prynne-Edwards—our Mr Prynne-Edwards—must have been. But I was rather surprised too, because I had thought that his Papa would be like his Mama, all shallow and stupid, and he would not be the sort of man that the iron-workers would choose to support.

"Have you heard the story, miss?" asked Mair, when I went to the kitchen later. "All about the race—ooh, terribly exciting, it was."

Her cousin Benny, who works at the Works, was one of the men who barricaded the gates and roads, it seems.

"They sat there yelling and shouting when they saw that Mr Roberts, looking like a sweating pig for all his fine clothes, sitting on his horse and screaming at them to get out of the road," said Mair, with her eyes like saucers. "That's what Benny told our mam, miss. But they wouldn't move, and Mr Roberts threatened them with his whip and cursed something awful, but they wouldn't shift. And then up comes Mr Prynne-Edwards, and such a cheer went up, our Benny said you could hear it in Llangoed and it was like the Queen was riding in. Mr Prynne-Edwards waved and smiled and thanked the men for their loyalty. Our Benny says he's a fair man, Mr Prynne-Edwards is."

April 9th

I went out into the garden this morning to see the rockery and everywhere budding with little flowers, the aubretia will soon be carpeting the steps with blossom, and the fragrance of rosemary drifting in the air. Mr Rochester accompanied me, tumbling down the steps on his short legs.

As we came up after our walk, I saw a horse coming along the drive, and I began to feel so strange, my heart beat very hard, and it was difficult to breathe. It was Mr Prynne-Edwards. At first I thought I could not face him—though why I should think that is a mystery, but when I came in, he was in the study with Father, talking very hard about Father's book and the Antiquarian Society, so Molly said.

"Did he ask for me?" I said, feeling hurt.

"Never a word," said Molly darkly.

I was so angry at his rudeness that I determined never to speak to him again and I wrapped my cloak around me and walked right down to the kitchen garden, determined to stay there until he had gone. I have never felt so furious, hurt and angry and miserable all at the same time. I felt like crying, but I was too angry to cry.

Then I heard footsteps coming down through the orchard, and it was him, looking so tall and handsome that I wanted to throw something at him.

"Good morning, Miss Roy," he said, and there was a light in his eyes that I hadn't seen before. "I have been talking to your father."

"I know," I answered rudely.

"I have asked his permission to marry you," he said, very directly. "He has given it." Then he looked straight into my eyes and said: "Will you marry me, Sophy?"

I could smell the warm herb scents coming stronger in the sun, and hear a lamb calling somewhere, and see the light catching the blue of his eyes and the curve of his cheek. I wanted to throw myself into his arms and sob out, oh yes, yes, of course and how miserable I had been and how much I loved him, but (it makes me go hot and embarrassed to remember it, fortunately this is a private diary) I snapped out that I could never think of such a thing, and turned away very much on my dignity.

"Why not?" he said, very persuasively, and he was so close to me that my heart was banging in a strange way, and I was very conscious of his coat sleeve brushing against me.

"I shall never marry," I said tragically. "I shall stay here and devote myself to Elvira or John Edward and my writing."

He turned me round gently, and when I saw the look on his face, I could not help myself, a frown came, and I said accusingly: "You are laughing at me."

"Indeed I'm not, Sophy. But your father has agreed—and my father approves of the match. Yes, he does. Mama and Clarissa have done their best to spoil things for us, but Papa is on my side. He admires you, he says you are a girl of unusual beauty and character."

I was so furious to think of his papa, whom I had imagined standing in the way of our getting married, turning out to be so easily won, that I felt a sob of sheer rage rising in my throat.

"I won't have Father giving people permission to marry me—without consulting me about it," I said, and he smiled and took my hands. "I have consulted you. I have asked you to marry me."

"I could never think of marrying anybody unless he was like—like Mr Rochester," I blurted.

"Mr Rochester?" He was plainly puzzled, because of course he only knows my guard dog who rolls on the floor to have his fur stroked.

"In Miss Brontë's book *Jane Eyre*," I said, feeling a malicious satisfaction. "He is the hero, he is dark and strange and oh, so fervent! You didn't even—." Here, to my horror, my voice trembled. "—You didn't even write to me. I have been so miserable."

I could tell that he was torn at this between laughing out loud and drawing me into his arms with the same fire as when he kissed me in the library, and I backed away, and said, almost without my own volition: "I could never marry a man who—who blushes!"

At this, he did laugh, with the humour brimming over in his eyes and I began to sob. "Go away," I said, into my hands. "I hate you." Then, as he still stood there, with his eyes full of laughter, I stamped my foot and shouted: "Go away—I never want to speak to you again."

He gave me a bow, very grave, but unable to hide the laughter.

"Madam," he said, and turned and went up through the orchard, still laughing. I felt so utterly, utterly wretched that I sat down on the old stone seat and sobbed.

April 10th

I was interrupted yesterday by Molly coming to call me for tea, and I could not add what happened after Mr Prynne-Edwards had gone. I sat and sobbed for a long time, and in the end, Father came down to the kitchen garden, looking quite pleased with himself. But his expression changed to surprise when he saw me.

"Why, Sophy!" he said, full of concern.

I could not help it. I threw myself into his arms (he is a lot taller than me) and sobbed into his shirt. "Oh, Father, how could I? I sent him away! I said I hated him—and I don't—and now he'll never know—"

"Tempest in a teacup," snorted Father, as I started weeping like a fountain once more. He took out his handkerchief, and handed it to me. "Come on, dry your eyes. It isn't the end of the world."

"But I love him, Father," I sobbed, wiping away at my face, which was all wet with tears. "And—now I shall never see him again—"

"You will, you know," said Father, and when I looked up, his eyes were twinkling. He looked rather like a naughty boy again, like he did when he brought Hélène home.

"I've invited him to the wedding—informally," he said, and after that there was no more need for me to cry.

It is amazing how much nearer I feel to Father since all the things that have happened lately. He pinched my cheek, when I was inclined to be tragic about Mr Prynne-Edwards, and said it takes more than that to keep a man in love away.

"I should know," he added, laughing.

"But Hélène didn't say she hated you," I protested.

"Only because there wasn't time," twinkled Father. "She knew I'd got a train to catch."

Hélène and her brother are coming on Wednesday, and Robert is to meet them with the carriage at the station. All their friends and associates in London are rather amazed that Hélène is not having a big fashionable wedding from her brother's house in London, but the attraction of our romantic private chapel is too strong, and neither Hélène nor Father wanted a big wedding anyway.

The Bishop and everybody will be staying here overnight on the night before because the wedding is quite early in the morning. Molly and the girls are in a great flutter at the idea of a bishop staying here, though Molly sniffed and said: "The Son of Man had no place to lay his head. What's good enough for Him ought to be good enough for a bishop." (This was when I was telling them to get the guest rooms ready.)

"We must be sociable. We can't expect the Bishop to sleep on the floor," I said, trying to hide my laughter.

April 11th

I dreamed last night about my mother. I dreamed that I was sleeping in my bedroom, but awake too and watching myself lying there with my hair in a thick black plait across the white coverlet, and then there was a movement at the door and the soft light of a candle, and my mother came in, dressed as she is in her portrait, in her dress of pale misty blue, with something glittering gold at her neck, and her black curls hanging on her shoulders. She came in and leaned over me, shielding the candle, and looked for a long while, and then she turned very quietly and went out. I knew in the dream that she was content and at peace, and she was happy that everything was well with me. I slept deeply after that, and woke refreshed this morning to a bright and sparkling day.

I looked out of my window before going down, at the chimneys of the farm and the sun warming the yard. The trees are beginning to fill out with budding leaves and hide the wall and the view over it from us. Shan came across the yard with eggs from the farm and I waved to her. She grinned very widely, but didn't wave back in case she dropped the eggs.

I came down this morning with a sense of expectation, as though something very pleasant is going to happen. Nothing has, in fact, but I still feel this delightful happy feeling spreading all through me, like sunlight itself, warming all the dark corners and sweeping out all the cobwebby places. I suppose it is the thought of Hélène coming and the excitement of the wedding.

In my mood of happy expectancy, I went out with Mr Rochester to walk in the garden in the sunshine, among the flowers. I think the gillyflowers are beginning to bloom. It is a sign that happiness is in store, that they should begin to bloom today. But I think I would have found everything a sign that happiness is in store.

Later

I tried to explain what I felt to Father at luncheon, and he looked sympathetic, but with the twinkle that is now almost constantly in his eyes.

"Ah! Rose-coloured spectacles," he said. "The result of falling in love, I imagine. Love is a great beautifier, Sophy."

I thought of Hélène's face as she looked when they came in from the Dyke, and I knew what he meant. In fact, though it is vain of me to stare at myself in the mirror, I looked at my own face when I went upstairs just now, and my face looks like Hélène's did that day. I feel beautiful all through, and my hair looks blacker and more glossy than ever, and my eyes are bright and my face looks glowing with a sort of light from within.

There is no doubt about it. I am in love. It is so wonderful, I feel as though I am walking on a cloud, and everything around me seems to be a part of the joyfulness. I feel as though I want to laugh and cry and run for miles across the park with my hair loose (except of course that the baby is too heavy now for me to run far).

How did I ever imagine that Mr Prynne-Edwards was not like a hero? He is more handsome than even the fashionable Edgar Linton in *Wuthering Heights* could have been, and I am sure it would not be half so pleasant to be kissed by Heathcliff or Jane Eyre's Mr Rochester, as it was when he kissed me in the library.

I feel very humble when I think how persistent he was, even though I kept on saying no and being rude to him. And how strong he must be—in his character, I mean—not to mind about the baby and the fact that I will be coming to him, as Clarissa put it so nastily, as "damaged goods".

"You are you, and I love you," he said in the orchard, on the day when I was not well, and he went to Staffordshire. When I think of that, I feel as though I must be very lovely and precious to him for him to care that much.

But I am even more glad that he wanted to marry me when I was just me in my old plaid dress and a fallen woman, and when nobody knew that I was going to be an heiress.

April 12th

Hélène is coming tomorrow, but this morning, Father suddenly declared he couldn't wait for her to arrive. He was all for travelling to London today, and bringing her back himself. It took the combined efforts of Molly and me and Doctor Hawk to stop him, but in the end he admitted that perhaps his idea had been a little wild.

I know how he feels, though. I woke this morning still in a happy frame of mind, but with such a sudden longing to see Mr Prynne-Edwards that I almost called for the carriage and went down to look for him at his home. How scandalized Clarissa and her mama would be if I turned up on the doorstep, in my condition, which is now quite obvious, and told them I had come to find Richard.

I have been going round today in a happy daze, but there has been so much to do that I have not been able to sit and think. The White Room, where we will be having the wedding breakfast, is shining after a good clean, the white ceiling reflecting colour today, changing rainbows of April light. The view outside the windows is all green now, the young fresh green of spring. It is beautiful to see after the bleak prospect I had from the same windows in the winter. Even the sundial in the middle of the lawn looks like a benevolent old friend, rather than a cold object of stone. And as for the chapel—Molly and the girls have been busy there, and the vicar and his people will be coming from the village soon to put the altar cloth and candles and the rest of the things out ready for the wedding.

I went out to look at the chapel when the girls had finished and stood for quite a long time inside the doorway, with the slanting sunlight making patterns of gold in the dimness inside.

The whole place has been cleaned from top to bottom, and the floor has been covered. Hélène's brother, the famous publisher, is to give her away. It is a pity her mother could not come. I would like to have met somebody who escaped from France during the Revolution.

I closed the door of the chapel quietly behind me and came back to the house, where Molly and Mair and Shan were working away for dear life. All the guest rooms are ready now, waiting for the Bishop and Hélène's brother and a famous portrait photographer from London who is to take their wedding picture (who is also going to stay overnight).

There is a feeling of expectancy through the house, a sort of waiting and listening, as though even the oak chest in the hall, and the paintings on the walls are holding their breath. It is just like it was before the ball, when I came down before the guests came. But this time, they are waiting for Hélène not for me.

I told Father he must have her portrait painted and put it in the drawing-room with my mother's. We stood together looking at my mother's sweet delicate face, and her wide dark eyes, and Father put his hand on my shoulder.

"You don't—mind, do you child?" he said, very seriously.

"No Father, truly. She is at peace and happy, I know it," I answered, and told him about my dream.

He nodded, and we looked up again at the painting, and my mother seemed to smile at us, and wish us well, Father and Hélène, and me and the baby, and Richard, and Molly and everybody here.

I came to sit out in the orchard in the sun to write today, with the blossom breaking into bloom all around, and to be out of the way of the cleaning. I have just looked up and seen Richard coming down the terrace steps.

Later

He said he could not wait until Friday, and we talked in the orchard for a long time, and he plaited a ring of grass to go round my finger until he can give me a gold one. Sitting here as the lamp burns quietly and the fire settles to sleep, I think I am the happiest person in the world. I fear I will not write in my diary very often in the future, I will be too busy telling Richard my thoughts instead of committing them to paper.

It will not be easy, I see that now. But I feel so brave and wise after talking to Richard that I think I can face it all. I will leave this house to Father and Hélène—their story is just beginning, but I must go out into the world before my new life can start. Tomorrow is a fateful day. Hélène will come here as the future mistress—and I will lift my eyes further than the garden, further than the park, the poplars, even my hills. Farewell to them all.

But I say it cheerfully. I will always be happy to return here, to visit the childhood house I have loved so much. But our future—the baby's and mine—is waiting somewhere beyond the gates at the end of the drive.

Where will our home be now? I do not know yet, but of one thing I am certain. I will go with him, I will love his family for his sake, and try to like Clarissa. I will have no regrets. For I love him with all my heart, and I will go with him gladly, wherever he chooses—even to the other side of the world.

April 13th

We had news today that Miss Brontë is dead, she died a week or two ago, it seems. It is a dreadful thing—I feel I should mourn, that the pen that wrote *Jane Eyre* is for ever stilled, and Miss Brontë is long since buried.

So how is it that I can feel so happy? . . .